# Life Threatened

By

Sandy Graham

**Books by Sandy Graham**

Pillage Trilogy
    Life Shattered
    Life Rescued
    Life Threatened

Murder – On Saltspring?
The Pizza Dough King
Speak For Me
A Quiet Rampage

Published in the United States of America

This is a work of fiction. Names, characters and incidents are the product of the author's imagination or are used fictitiously. Any resemblance to actual persons, living or dead, or events is entirely coincidental.

Copyright © 2021 by Sandy Graham
All rights reserved.

ISBN: 9798458234795

# Dedication

To my family, immediate and extended, including by marriage and adoption. You all enjoy a sense of humour that guarantees gatherings spiced with joyful entertainment. Some of you are exceptionally gifted—no, all are gifted in various ways. Most important, you are caring.

My parents lived by the Golden Rule and the gold they received in return took the form of friendships. Some combination of genetics and education managed to pass that orientation on. You are givers, not takers.

In a world where hate foments hate, caring begets caring. Perhaps that is the underlying message in this book. I long for a world dominated by caring families like you that can lead us back to universal civility.

# Author's Note

This story was originally published under the title "Two Loves Challenged" which apparently led some to expect a romance novel. It is a literary novel which crosses the genres of romance, adventure and historical fiction.

# Chapter 1

The young couple, happy and carefree, held hands as they strolled the three blocks from the Queen E Theatre to their parking lot. Pam softly sang her favorite song from the concert. Tom hummed along. Two men meandered from side to side on the sidewalk as they approached. They obviously spent time in the beer parlour behind them. Plotting the men's course as best they could, Tom and Pam moved to one side to let them pass. The shorter of the two veered directly into Pam.

"Hey Babe. I'd like to screw you."

Tom spoke up, "Leave us alone."

"Or what?"

With no warning, his fist slammed into Tom's face, broke his nose and sent him sprawling backwards. His head banged hard on the sidewalk. If he wasn't unconscious on the way down, the sidewalk ended any doubt. Pam screamed. Tried to come between them. The man hit her with a sweeping backhand that flung her up against a building.

"I'll deal with you later, bitch."

He stepped forward and delivered a kick to the side of Tom's head that slammed it into his left shoulder. It stayed pressed against the shoulder at an impossible angle. The blood flowing from his nose was joined by a trickle from the ear. Pam screamed again. His partner grabbed his arm.

"Jobo, he aint moving. Maybe you killed him."

"Bastard won't cross me again."

"C'mon Jobo, we got to get the hell out of here."

Jobo gave Tom another kick before letting his big partner drag him away to their car. As they left, Pam bent down over Tom. He didn't move.

"Tom! No! Tom!"

She screamed for help. No one in sight. She screamed again and again.

Another couple rounded the corner, saw the girl bent over the boy and ran to help. The woman sized up the situation immediately.

"Run to the pub and have them call the police and an ambulance."

She knelt beside Pam.

"Straighten his head gently and lower it to the pavement. Hold it steady. Pull slightly."

She felt for a pulse in his carotid arteries. None detected. She put her ear close to his mouth. No sign of breathing. With one hand helping Pam hold his head steady, she stuck a finger in his mouth to pull the tongue forward, then put her mouth on his and blew. His chest expanded. Moving over his chest, she placed the heel of both hands on his ribs and pressed down hard six times to pump blood. Back to his mouth for another breath. Six more presses. She kept on though it became obvious he was gone. Tears streamed down Pam's face. She kept repeating, "No. No. No…"

Agonized minutes passed before they heard a siren. The patrol car screeched to a stop beside them. Two Mounties jumped out.

"Are you getting any response?"

"No."

She straightened up and wiped the blood from around her mouth, felt for a pulse one last time knowing full well there wouldn't be one.

"We should continue until a medic arrives."

"I just graduated from medical school. It's no use. He's gone."

Pam became hysterical and the girl held her, tried to calm her down. They cried together. A Mountie put his arm gently on her shoulder.

"Please give me your name."

"Cynthia Adams."

Onlookers seemed to materialize from both directions. The second officer told them to stay back.

"This is a crime scene. Move back. If any of you saw anyone suspicious leaving the area, stay until we get your information. The rest of you go on about your business."

A few reluctantly left. Many remained to gawk as an ambulance pulled up. A medic leaped out. The Mountie signalled him to stop, they were too late. His partner went back to the patrol car and radioed for a crime investigation team. Pam was in shock.

Cynthia said, "She should be taken to Emergency."

"We'll take her," the medic responded.

"I want to stay with Tom!"

"I'm very sorry, Ma'am, it's too late to help Tom now. But you can help us find his killer."

She turned her tear stained face to him, stared for a moment to regain awareness of the situation, then nodded slightly.

"First, what's your name?"

"Pam Emerson."

"And your friend's?"

"Tom Newell."

"Can you tell me what happened?"

Between sobs, "…Two drunks came toward us. We moved to let them by…One came at me, threatened me…Tom told him to leave us alone. He suddenly punched Tom so hard he fell backward and hit his head on the sidewalk…"

She broke down again. Cynthia held and comforted her.

"…Then he kicked Tom on the side of his head hard…he had heavy boots on. Tom never moved. His partner pulled him off. Said they had to get away. He kicked Tom again before they left."

"Can you describe them?"

"The bad one was shorter than Tom. He wore a wool plaid shirt and jeans held up by suspenders instead of a belt. I didn't look at the other one except he was very big."

"Anything else you can tell us? Did you see the car they left in?"

"No. I heard them peel rubber on the street."

"Anything else?"

"No…oh, his partner called him Jobo."

# Chapter 2

Delbert Pillage rolled his wheelchair to the front door as his wife Sylvia carried the suitcase and overnight bag to the car. She slid them in behind the front seat. Delbert locked the door and rolled to her. After he heaved himself into the passenger seat, she folded his wheelchair and stowed it in the trunk.

When she settled behind the wheel Delbert asked, "Why do you insist on driving when we're together?"

"Perhaps for the same reason you insist on piloting the airplane. It gives me something to do."

"There's so few times when I get the car on my own, it was hardly worth converting it to hand controls."

"It was one more project for you to tackle. For a while, I was afraid I would have to roll into the driving position in a wheel chair too."

He laughed, "Very funny."

Sylvia was resigned to the fact he always needed the challenge of a project. When he first brought up the idea, the thought had crossed her mind that a reduction in time spent ferrying him around might be welcome. As it turned out, he drove himself around much more than he now let on.

Delbert mused aloud, "Hard to believe it's almost eight years since we found Thia sitting in the gutter."

"Who'd have thought she would become a doctor back then?"

"Hard to guess, even though she was obviously bright and showed great strength of character once the methadone took effect."

"It's wonderful that she's weaned herself off it without regression."

"For sure."

Sylvia drove them to Langford Lake where their flying boat was moored. Flying boat was an apt description for Delbert's creation. Built on top of a Boston Whaler hull, the plane was propelled by two large industrial fans driven from a completely muffled Volkswagen engine. All one could hear inflight was the woosh of air from the fans.

Fondly called "Delboat" by air traffic controllers and friends, it was designed to silently spy on drug smugglers operating in Northwest waters. In fact, it proved instrumental in breaking up a smuggling ring. In the years since, Delbert's periodic surveillance had discouraged other attempts to set up a new operation.

With no wind, the lake was a sheet of glass. Delbert rolled down onto the float and unlocked the dockside door, which was in two pieces, hinged top and bottom. The top half with windows swung up to provide a sheltered entry when it rained. The bottom half dropped down to form a platform if stopped at the horizontal position or became a ramp if allowed to drop further.

There were two seats on the far side of the cabin, none on the near side. Sylvia carried the suitcases on board and stowed them behind the rear seat. Delbert rolled up the ramp, turned and rolled forward to the controls, then locked the wheelchair in position. He powered up the airplane as Sylvia closed the doors and cast off the mooring lines.

He used the steerable water jet to pull away from the dock, turn the plane around and take it back in. Sylvia opened the passenger side door, climbed into the front seat and closed the door again.

As he taxied out, Delbert started the engine. Sylvia read off checklist items while it warmed up. Then Delbert advanced the throttle, the fans spun up and they began the takeoff run. Liftoff occurred at sixty knots and they climbed silently into the sky. Delbert swung north toward Vancouver and contacted air traffic control to file a flight plan.

"I never tire of flying this beautiful old girl."

"I'm jealous. You never call me a beautiful old girl."

"That's because you're a beautiful young woman."

"Do you sometimes wish you were back in a jet fighter?"

"No...oh, occasionally, I suppose. No, not really. I don't like to dwell on things like that."

She chuckled, "You've managed to live a pretty full life since the accident all things considered."

"For the most part. I'm glad you became a public health nurse. It's fun flying you into the reservation villages up island."

"Fun for me too. And satisfying to help people out."

They flew over the gulf islands and headed across the Strait of Georgia. His plan was to skirt the airport controlled airspace and land in Vancouver Harbour. Cynthia had agreed to meet them at the Seaplane Flight Centre and drive them to their hotel.

Over English Bay Delbert broke the silence again, "Hope Thia's there when we arrive."

"You know she's always punctual."

"And meticulous. She'll make a great doctor. Course punctuality will shock most patients."

"Watching her get her degree will bring a thrilling climax to her journey from teen drug addict to doctor."

"We can be proud both of her and our contribution to help make it happen. Hope I have a chance to spend a little time with Dean Calder while we're here."

Delbert turned the airplane into what wind there was and descended smoothly to the water. He left the engine running to taxi in. Within coasting distance of the dock, he deployed the water jet and cut the engine. The water jet allowed him to maneuver the plane as easily as a boat. After letting Sylvia off on the dock, he turned the plane around and docked on his side. Sylvia tied the mooring lines.

With everything shut off and the airplane buttoned up, they started up the dock, Sylvia with the bags, Delbert rolling behind. Cynthia waved to them from the top of the ramp. When they reached her, the two women hugged. Cynthia bent over the chair to hug Delbert.

"Let me take the suitcases, Mum."

"I can handle them."

Cynthia had already wrestled one out of her hand. Sylvia studied her informally adopted daughter on the way to the hotel.

"You seem a little subdued, Thia. Are you nervous about the ceremony tomorrow?"

"No...It's impossible to keep a secret from you two. Last night I stumbled onto a gruesome scene. For no reason at all, a man murdered a teenager by punching and kicking him. It was ghastly."

"Couldn't anyone stop him?"

"There was just the victim's girlfriend and the murderer's partner. It all happened just before we saw them. Don't think the police have found the murderer, probably never will. All they know is what he wore and his name is Jobo."

"That's horrible!"

Delbert interjected, "What was he wearing?"

"A plaid wool shirt and jeans held up by suspenders instead of a belt."

"And boots. Sounds like a farmer or logger."

"The girl said he was short and his partner was a big man."

"A sociopath with short man syndrome — and the big man didn't want to stop him…or couldn't?"

"Perhaps it happened too fast."

# Chapter 3

An atmosphere of excitement permeated the auditorium. Chatter and laughter everywhere as proud students and prouder parents waited for the festivity to begin. And when it did, even the Dean of Medicine's rather dry commencement address, with all the usual platitudes, did nothing to dampen enthusiasm and anticipation.

As each gowned graduate filed up and across the stage, a portion of the crowd applauded when the student's name was announced and the rolled degree presented. Delbert and Sylvia joined in when Cynthia's turn arrived. Unlike others who filed back down off the stage, Cynthia moved to a row of chairs at the rear.

Sylvia whispered, "Why did she do that?"

"She must have some other duty to perform later."

Since Adams was near the front of the alphabet, they were a long time waiting for an explanation. Finally, James Zimmerman's name came up and the procession ended. The dean stepped back to the microphone.

"We will now have the valediction, presented by Doctor Cynthia Adams."

Both Delbert and Sylvia felt a lump in their throats as Cynthia walked to the podium.

"Thank you, Dean Ferguson and all faculty members. How many times over the past four years did you wonder if you could possibly get us to this point? Well, you succeeded and here we are, fellow classmates. HERE WE ARE!"

When the cheer died down, she continued, "Most of us experienced moments of doubt along the way. The road was bumpy, the hills steep, the way often foggy. Yet somehow, with help from a caring staff and each other, we made it to this day.

"When Tommy watched the first slice into a cadaver and woke up on the floor, we all laughed but we helped him up. I have no doubt that he is in the process of becoming one of the finest surgeons around. And when Sally first appeared in her lab coat with a name tag over her left breast and George asked her what she called the other one, even Sally laughed. As our professors instilled in us, a doctor must have a thick skin, a quick wit and a slick tongue. We've enjoyed four years of experiences and escapades which will be remembered for a lifetime.

"And along the way we have learned so much—about medicine, about suffering, about treatment, about ourselves. We are such different people today from those who entered four years ago as to be unrecognizable without a face to home in on.

"I can't resist relating a little of my personal journey in this respect. For those unaware, eight years ago I was a teenage drug addict literally rescued from the gutter by my adoptive parents, Delbert and Sylvia Pillage. As much as I fought them those first months, they persisted to get me on methadone and remained a pillar of love to bring me back to life. I feel that love every day and marvel at how far it has brought me to stand now amongst my fellow classmates as the doctors of tomorrow.

"For that's what we are, doctors who will fan out into widespread communities to help the afflicted, treat the sick, heal the wounded, always with the compassion so often stressed here. We are the product of your dedication, our beloved staff—sometimes held in trepidation but always in respect. How often did we wonder if we would dare step into a hospital? Now we look forward to it with a confidence you have instilled in us. We thank you. We thank you so much!"

The applause that accompanied her as she joined her classmates was loud and heartfelt. Neither Delbert nor Sylvia could speak. Their hearts were in their throats. Tears leaked from their eyes. The pride they felt in Cynthia overpowered them.

The Dean thanked Cynthia, added a few closing remarks and wished the class bon voyage. Graduates began searching for parents and friends. Delbert and Sylvia managed to stem their emotions by the time Cynthia found them. They hugged.

"We didn't know you were to be valedictorian. What an honour! You did a magnificent job."

Sylvia added, "We're so proud of you, Thia!"

Cynthia responded, "I can never stress enough how much you two have meant to me. I owe my life to you."

Delbert decided to defuse the returning emotion, "We'll drown in mutual admiration if we're not careful."

"Good old Dad, always trying to keep an even keel," Cynthia laughed.

"Is your class having a party this evening?"

"Yes, but there'll be a lot of drinking. I think it prudent to skip it."

A sobering thought passed through each parent's mind. Cynthia remained concerned that she might have an addictive personality, perhaps with valid grounds. They decided on a celebratory dinner alone instead.

Dean Calder intercepted them on the way out.

"Delbert, Sylvia, did you think you could sneak into town and out again without saying hello?"

"Of course not, Dean. I planned to camp on your doorstep tomorrow."

"Cynthia, I snuck in the back to hear your address. You did a wonderful job, dear."

"Thank you, Dean. It was an unexpected honour."

"We are planning a quiet dinner together, Dean. Would you care to join us?"

"Don't want to horn in."

"We would love you to join us. In a very real sense you are responsible for starting our lives down the path we have enjoyed. You and the Martins."

"I was talking to Dan yesterday. We reminisced about our times with you."

"I should have called him. We didn't know what Thia would want to do this evening, so it was hard to make plans."

"Why not call him now. Maybe he and Samantha could join us—unless we're crashing your dinner party."

Delbert went off in search of a phone while the other three continued to chat. He returned in less than ten minutes.

"Dan recommended a fine restaurant. We agreed to meet there at seven."

# Chapter 4

Two men sat in the green Monarch convertible waiting for the ferry at Horseshoe Bay.

"Nothing on the news. Maybe he's still alive."

"Who cares?"

"You should, Jobo. If he's dead they'll look for a murderer."

"Listen, asshole. I'm not going to tell you again. Stop calling me Jobo. My name's Joe. Understand?"

"I like Jobo."

"Knock it off unless you want to wind up like that punk last night."

Ned laughed, "You and what army, squirt?"

"You may be a big fucker. That just means you'll fall harder. Don't test me, man."

Ned looked down at the cold, snake-like eyes that bored into him. The involuntary shudder they provoked made him think twice.

"Okay, Joe, have it your way. Probably smarter to put Jobo to rest. I might've called you that last night on the sidewalk."

"How much longer before that boat shows up?"

Ned glanced at his watch, "About twenty minutes."

"Sooner we get back on the Island and out of sight the better. If he died they'll be looking for a big oaf and me. Probably check all the ferry traffic."

"Funny you should say that. There's a Mountie way down at the front of the line."

"Shit! Get out and go to the crapper. Then board as a foot passenger. I'll drive the car on."

"You sure we need to do that?"

"Go!"

Joe slid behind the wheel and watched the Mountie stroll up the line. He didn't ask questions. Just a casual glance at each car. *The punk must have kicked the bucket.* He tried to look calm but his stomach was a tangled mass of butterflies. Not much scared him but going back to the pen did. It took all his willpower to lean back and close his eyes in a fake nap. He expected a tap on the window at any moment but it didn't come.

*Has he passed? Can't tell.* As the minutes ticked by, he gained confidence. When there was no doubt, he pretended to wake up and look around to see if the ferry had arrived, then fake a yawn. After that ritual, he couldn't resist a glance in the mirror. The cop had finished his two lanes and headed back down the next pair. He was going to make it onto the boat which just now came in sight.

Fifteen minutes later the Mountie stood on the driver's side of the ramp as cars boarded. Joe automatically glanced at him. Their eyes met briefly. Joe forced a slight smile which the cop acknowledged. He made it onboard.

It took another twenty-five minutes for Ned to find his car. He opened the driver's door and told Joe to slide across.

"You owe me fifteen bucks for the extra ticket."

"It's worth it. That cop was definitely searching for a pair like us."

"There could be someone on this tub too."

"Doubt it...but if it makes you feel better I'll lie down in the back under that blanket you carry around."

Joe scanned the cars around them to make sure no one watched while he climbed into the back. It was hard to get comfortable with the driveshaft hump in the middle, but he made the best of it and pulled the blanket over him. Ned reached back and straightened it out.

"Hey asshole, crack a window. It's hot down here."

Ned complied. "If you want me to call you Joe, start using my name too."

"Okay, ass—Ned."

Stuck in the car, it took forever to reach Departure Bay. Eventually they did and Ned drove off without incident. As soon as they were well on their way north on the Island Highway, Joe climbed back into the front seat. Refreshed by the cool air, he laughed.

"Wonder if they were after us? Could be anything. There's been nothing on the news."

"Just the same, I'll be glad to be back in camp until it blows over."

"You know, more I think about it, seems like we should assume two things."

"What?"

"He's dead and they're looking for us."

"Looking for you, you mean."

"No, us. The best clue they have is there was a big oaf and a regular guy with him."

"Yeah, that's the long and the short of it," Ned said with a laugh.

Joe bristled, "You call me short again and I'll look tall next to what's left of you."

"Take it easy, Joe. Just making a little joke. Geez, you're touchy."

"Screw you. Thing is, we got to go separate ways for a while. Drop me off at Mabel's and get a plane back to camp on Saturday. I'll fly up on Sunday."

An hour later they neared Campbell River. Ned asked Joe to remind him where Mabel lived.

"On Dogwood. Turn left on Second."

Ned watched Mabel open the door. *She's a little shorter than Joe but she's got a body that won't quit. Lucky bastard. Don't know what she sees in him.* Joe turned and waved Ned away. Mabel waved too. Then they disappeared inside. Ned drove down to the Quinsam Hotel to drown his loneliness in beer.

Unlike Joe, Ned's big frame enabled him to chug beer for hours without significant effect. If anything, he turned into a big likeable bear, the soft kind, not the mean ones that showed up in the logging area at times

# Chapter 5

Delbert and Dan Martin shook hands with enthusiasm and embraced each other's wife. Sylvia and Samantha hugged as well. The Martins turned to Cynthia with congratulations on her accomplishment. Dean Calder smiled as he watched the greetings and reminisced in his mind once again about the long roads each had traveled to reach this happy point.

Seated with drinks ordered, the process of catching up began. As guest of honour, attention turned first to Cynthia. Dan asked about her near-term plans.

"I've been offered an internship in Campbell River for next year. Haven't made plans beyond that yet."

"Do you expect to specialize?"

"Not at this moment. I prefer the role of general physician. It keeps me in initial contact with people needing medical help. That may change if I'm swamped with hypochondriacs."

They laughed. Dean Calder said, "That's an interesting and noble viewpoint. So many want to limit their patients by specializing and I think they spend most of their time bored by performing the same procedures over and over. Of course, some simply go after the higher fees."

"If there's an advantage to living through the seedier side of life, it motivates one to help others avoid or recover from it."

That caused an emotional silence as each thought back on Cynthia's youth. Some eyes became a little teary. True to form, Delbert broke the silence.

"We now have two family members in the health care business. I can get sick at will and know I'll be looked after."

Sylvia rose to the bait, "Poor dear, had it so hard before."

Dan interjected, "Are you a nurse again, Sylvia, not that you haven't nursed roller-boy for years?"

"Yes, Delbert became so independent I had to go back to school out of boredom. I'm a Public Health Nurse now."

"Great," Samantha threw in, "Are you practicing it in the Victoria area?"

"Not really. I cover the west coast of the island from Metchosin all the way up to Gold River."

"That's some rugged country."

"Delbert flies me into the remote areas. It's fun except he has to wait for me a lot. He's figured out a way to fish for salmon using Delboat."

Dan couldn't resist, "Do you land them or air them, Delbert?"

"You make fun. I caught a thirty-one pound Tyee last week."

Sylvia continued, "We're thinking of moving to Campbell River. There's a need for nurses to visit the remote tribal communities up the coast as well as on the Island."

"Does that mean you will give up your professorship, Delbert?"

"At Vic College. I might do some teaching or tutoring in Campbell River or Courtenay. And I'll be Sylvia's air taxi."

"So you're still flying Delboat?"

"We flew over in it."

"Who maintains it for you?"

"It doesn't need much maintenance. I've got a mechanic who is an expert on VW engines and once a year we con Jack into coming over and checking the rest of it. He's always surprised to find it in perfect working order."

"Still looking for smugglers?"

"Periodically. It's quiet these days. Think we've scared them away from the water route. We did catch a new operation last year. During the summer, I try to spot forest fires."

"It's his excuse to get flying time," Sylvia added.

"Incidentally," Dan said, "You're not the only one of us with a seaplane now."

"What do you mean?"

"I traded in my old friend for a Cessna one eighty-five on floats. I really enjoy the freedom from airports. Every lake and bay is an available destination."

Dean Calder entered the conversation, "You never go long without a project, Delbert. What is it now?"

Delbert laughed, "Well, if you must know, I'm toying with the idea of designing a system to fly planes in place of the pilot."

"Pilotless flight?"

"Yes and no. There's two parts that interest me. One is automatic control of an airplane throughout a flight, with a pilot onboard to manage it. The second would be a vehicle that could carry passengers without a pilot."

Dan piped up, "Won't that take all the fun out of flying?"

"Only if one lets it. What it would do is remove drudgery and it could eliminate navigation errors."

"Sounds ambitious."

"That's Delbert's forte," Dean Calder threw in.

"Well, it would be great if you can involve some of our engineering students to help with the electronics."

"I won't hesitate to suggest projects for them. They've been win-win in the past."

The conversation turned back to the Martins. Samantha revealed that their son Charlie and his wife Virginia were the proud parents of a third child, a second girl. Their eldest, Del, turned nine and was a soccer star already.

Often animated, topic followed topic. Eventually everyone was caught up and dessert and coffee consumed. The party broke up in the parking lot with hugs, handshakes and promises to get together more often.

Sylvia studied Cynthia as she drove them back to the hotel. "You seemed pensive, even sad, at times tonight, Thia. Are you sorry to leave college?"

"No. I hoped it didn't show but I keep thinking of Pam and Tom. It was horrible, so senseless, so final."

"A person who does that must be a psychopath," Delbert mused, "Incapable of empathy toward another human being—or animal for that matter."

"How can they feel that way?"

"That's just it, they don't feel. I've always been interested in how the brain works. There's research out now that addresses your question."

"What?"

"It explains how we empathize with each other using body language. Their studies show that when someone smiles at you, for example, your facial muscles automatically form a miniscule version of a smile. The nerves sense it and transmit the result to the brain to signal happiness. Or it might be a frown, grimace, gasp or whatever. We learn how someone else feels by an imperceptible imitation of them.

"Psychopaths are unable to mimic the expression nor get the signal to their brain, so they simply don't feel what others feel and have no empathy for them as a result."

"Sounds like you're making an excuse for them."

"No, not at all. Though I read of one case where a man with the problem was taught how to read, at least in part, people's expressions and learn when they felt happiness, pain, fear and so on. Guess it only happened because he became aware that he was missing something and wanted to learn. There's a side-note you might be interested in as a doctor, Thia."

"What is it?"

"Some doctors are beginning to combat aging and wrinkles by deadening facial nerves with a chemical called Botox. In the process, they in effect kill the patient's ability to empathize."

"Creating psychopaths?"

"I wouldn't go that far but they do lose their ability to detect what others feel."

Sylvia changed the subject, "Will it bother you if we move to Campbell River?"

"No. That would be great. Why should it?"

"You're at an age when you might want to be more independent from us. Of course, you can live in your own place."

"Will I not be welcome in yours?" She laughed.

"We can never see enough of you. You know that."

"I know. Let's cross that bridge when the time comes. I decided to take the position there before you mentioned the possibility of moving. Since I will be there first, I'll find an apartment to rent for the time being."

"Perhaps you will find some young friends to share an apartment."

"Perhaps."

\* \* \*

Cynthia gave them a tour of the university in the morning before stopping for lunch in English Bay and returning them to the dock. On the flight back to Victoria, Sylvia asked, "Do you think we'll be horning in on Thia in Campbell River?"

"I wonder about that. She'll be there first and like she says will rent an apartment. Whether she stays in the apartment or moves back in with us is her choice. "

"We need to make sure we don't cause her to feel an obligation to move in."

"Yes. Or an obligation not to as well. Of course, we could move to Comox instead."

"I don't favor that. The coastal health services are co-ordinated out of Campbell River."

"Then we'll rely on Thia to do what she wants."

# Chapter 6

Ned spent Sunday wandering around town. He felt estranged from Jobo or Joe as he now had to call him. The scene in Vancouver haunted him. Was the kid dead? He bought a Vancouver Sun and scanned it for word on the incident. Nothing. He noticed Obituaries in the column index and turned to that page.

Most were old people. Then one caught his eye:

> Newell, Thomas James. Age 19. Died too young of undisclosed cause. Tom will be remembered and loved by all who knew him. Survived by parents James and Martha Newell and sister Agatha.

*That could be him. Didn't she call him Tom as we left? I think so. Shit! Jobo—Joe must have killed him.*

"Died too young" caused his stomach to churn. He told himself it happened so fast he couldn't stop it. Perhaps he could have come between Joe and them as they approached. It was so unnecessary, so senseless. He wondered why he palled around with Jobo. *He really is a mean, heartless bastard but he's the only friend I have. Is he really a friend? Does he consider me a friend? That's more to the point. Would he stand by me the way I back him?*

The rest of the day was a struggle for Ned. He had to fight down waves of guilt. Over and over, he convinced himself there was nothing he could have done. The thought that he should go to the police preyed on him. He told himself that wouldn't bring the kid back to life. It wouldn't do any good.

At four in the afternoon he showed up at the seaplane dock for his scheduled flight back to the logging camp. Action and contact with others allowed him to shove aside the issue.

Joe greeted him in the mess tent with a laugh as though nothing had happened.

"Hey Ned. You get laid last night?"

"Nah, just had a few beers at the Quinsam with the usual gang."

The talk turned to logging. This site was almost logged off and the foreman let them know they would be moving camp about a mile further up the sound.

"When?" Someone asked.

"Later this month. There's a crew in there cutting spar trees now and the first dozer will work its way up this week."

After dinner, Ned motioned Joe to bring a beer outside. They sat on a log and watched the sun move down toward the hills on the far side of the sound. Joe broke the silence.

"Something bugging you, Ned?"

Ned glanced around to be sure no one watched. "There's an obituary in the Sun that looks like the kid's."

"How do you know? Did it say he died in a fight?"

"Died too young of undisclosed cause."

"Could be anybody. Anyway, what's the difference?"

"Guess it's too late to make a difference except it means you need to be extra careful until it blows over."

"You mean we need to, Ned. You're in this too and don't forget it. Don't go blab to somebody when you're drunk."

"I can hold my beer and my tongue, Joe."

Joe bristled, "Are you saying I can't?"

"Forget it."

Ned got up and walked towards the bunkhouse. Joe watched him leave and wondered for the first time if he could trust his partner.

# Chapter 7

Sylvia hung up the phone. "Charlie, Virginia and the kids are in Vancouver. They want to come over on Friday for the weekend."

"Great. Assume they're driving and taking the ferry."

"They expect to arrive around two."

*　*　*

Charlie and Virginia sported enviable tans. Little Del, antsy and excited, yet restrained by the new surroundings, glanced curiously at Delbert's wheelchair. His sister half hid behind her mother. The grown-ups hugged while the children watched. A cry from the car reminded them the baby wanted attention. Virginia retrieved her with Sylvia helping to carry in the things she needed.

Delbert turned to the boy. "How would you like to go flying tomorrow with Charlie and me?"

Del nodded, "I'd like to."

Charlie chimed in, "Delbert, you know how I hate flying. You two can go. Maybe Virginia would like to join you."

Delbert laughed. "For someone who is afraid of nothing, you still shy away from heights."

"It's not the height, it's the empty space between airplane and ground. Wouldn't be a problem if there was a mountain there."

"That might prove to be a problem for the airplane."

Charlie chuckled. "Anyway, I only fly when there's no alternative."

* * *

Once the children were in bed, the four parents talked over old times. Sylvia asked Virginia how she managed to stay so fit and trim.

"The kids keep me hopping but what really helps is running every day. Why don't we run together in the morning?"

"I could never keep up with you. And what about the baby?"

"Charlie will look after her, won't you dear?"

"Sure. Any excuse not to get pressured into flying."

"Will Del and Sammi go with me?"

"Del certainly will. He asked if we thought Uncle Delbert would take him up off and on all week. Sammi's shy but she's an adventuresome little devil so she'll be game too."

* * *

Del's excitement sagged a little when he saw Delboat. It was not like any airplane he had ever seen. Delbert caught his apprehension and told him it was a great flying machine with hours and hours in the air. The kids climbed over the aisle stand into the two seats as Delbert wheeled onboard and cast off the mooring lines. He showed Del how to move the seat forward so he could reach the controls and then to buckle his seatbelt. Del's excitement revived.

It was harder to get Sammi to buckle in but soon she was sitting in quiet anticipation, barely able to see over the window sill. After going through the pre-start checklist, Delbert raised the ramp and they moved away from the dock. When he started the engine, Del asked why there wasn't any noise. Delbert said it was designed to be very quiet but not to worry, the engine was running fine. He pointed to the RPM gage to prove it.

Excitement mounted as they picked up speed and lifted off. Del said "Wow" and Delbert noticed even Sammi now wore a smile. Delbert named the Gulf Islands as they passed over them.

"That's Salt Spring Island where Sylvia and I were born and grew up."

"Look at the cliff," Del exclaimed.

"That's Mount Maxwell."

Delbert's mind traveled back to the time he and Sylvia first made love there. The only time they made love before he was paralyzed. It took an effort to pull himself out of his sudden melancholy mood. Del sensed it and remained quiet.

"Want to fly the plane, Del?"

"I don't know how."

"I'll show you. Grasp the joystick gently. That's it. Now move it slowly to the left. See how the wing banks and puts us into a turn. Let the joystick go back to center. We just stay in the turn. To straighten out, you move it to the right until the wings are level again. That's it."

As the lesson continued, Del proved to be a quick learner. Within ten minutes, he knew how to check for traffic and then turn smoothly to the heading requested. Delbert supplied the power and rudder corrections to keep the turns co-ordinated.

The boy was so adept he decided to show him how to do that too. It seemed appropriate to tell him most airplanes had rudder pedals rather than his dual-purpose throttle and rudder control joystick.

"Why don't they just have one of these? Bet it's easier to use."

Delbert smiled. "Perhaps it is once you get the hang of it. However, there's some complicated electrical equipment needed behind the scenes."

Although it looked like Del would be happy to spend the rest of the day aloft, Sammi showed signs of boredom after an hour, so they headed back to Langford Lake. Both kids were thrilled with the splashdown. Delbert cut the engine and showed them how to control the water jet. Del was soon taxiing across the lake.

"Let Sammi try it."

His reluctance was overwhelmed by her enthusiasm. Tentative at first, she soon had them doing figure eights with a little more speed than Delbert preferred.

"Okay Sammi, steer for that dock," he commanded, pointing to their float.

"How fast will it go?"

"Push the handle all the way forward and we'll find out."

Left to her own, it looked like Sammi would run it up on the beach. Delbert took over. Back at the house, the kids gave an excited rendition of their whole excursion.

"We even saw where you were born, Aunt Sylvia. And Mount Maxwell."

Sylvia glanced involuntarily at her husband. Both knew what the other was thinking.

Virginia broke in, "We ran along your route this morning. Sylvia moves right out."

"I'll probably pay for it tomorrow."

* * *

By Tuesday morning, Sylvia was ready to run with Delbert on his morning route.

"You don't need to wait for me. Go at your usual pace."

"No, we'll go at yours, today at least."

That proved to be so much slower than usual that Delbert realized they would have to train separately in future. But for today, it gave them a chance to talk.

"Virginia spoke to Cynthia last week. She's still bothered by that murder."

"What makes a man do that?"

"Virginia attributes it to a need for dominance that modern man feels."

"Guess I'm not modern."

"You're just not caught up in it and many men aren't. She says that back in the hunter-gatherer day both sexes played an equal part in finding food for survival. Often, it was the females who decided when and where to move. When human population exceeded what earth could support with that lifestyle, farming and animal husbandry became necessary. Then the man's role transitioned from hunter to property defender and male dominance was born."

"How so?"

"There are three main ingredients to property: fertile land, herds and breeding females. Women became chattel instead of partners."

"Suppose so."

"It happened at different times in various locations but generally about five thousand years ago. That dominance has led to centuries of wars, violence and brutality."

"That's certainly true, more to women than men."

"That's what Virginia said."

Delbert rolled to a stop in front of a small grocery store where a man was arranging vegetables on a stand out front. Sylvia welcomed the respite.

"Hi Mario. Fine day."

"Delberto! How you doing today?"

"Great. Looks like the kohlrabi is in season at last."

"Good kohlrabi. You want some?"

Delbert glanced at Sylvia. She nodded.

"Sure, we'll take two."

"How you get such beautiful company, Delberto?"

"This is my wife, Sylvia."

Mario bowed slightly. "Your acquaintance is enchanting, Signora."

"It's a pleasure to meet you, Mario. Does Delbert stop here often?"

"Almost every day, Signora." Delbert laughed.

"Since he seems to like that kohlrabi, perhaps you can tell me how to cook it?"

"Ah, si. You cut it into little cubes and boil them until they are soft. On the plate, you add butter and pepper."

After paying, the kohlrabi was deposited in Delbert's lap and they were off again.

"So, Virginia thinks males were not always dominant?"

"No, if anything it was the other way around. In fact, she claims anthropologists suggest that males themselves are a fairly recent introduction in terms of life on earth."

"What?"

"Think about it. Early life forms were all single sex. She says that species that developed male and female sexes did so to create genetic variation. It was needed to make evolution and survival of the fittest work."

"That part I understand."

"She says the human embryo is essentially the female form of human at first. The Y chromosome genes that determine it will be male convert what would otherwise become ovaries into testis. They create the hormones—androgens—that build male features and suppress female ones."

"You mean males are chemically grown out of female eggs?"

"Guess that's one way to put it."

"Kind of puts down us males. We're only around to give genetic diversity."

"Don't worry dear, you males are good for more than that."

"You mean for entertainment?"

She laughed. "That too. I was thinking more of the support role you play throughout life."

"Suppose male dominance comes about because some of us are not content with a support role."

"That murderer, Jobo, certainly wasn't."

Both became somber. "I still think he also suffers from an inability to read people's emotions."

Delbert rolled to a stop beside a school yard and watched a bunch of youngsters playing soccer. Glad for another rest, Sylvia leaned against the wheelchair with a hand on his shoulder.

As he watched, memories flooded back. A scrawny kid who could have been him at that age hovered near the sideline. He couldn't resist a yell at the ball-hog to pass to his wing. Sylvia applied a calming pressure on his shoulder. After losing the ball, the big kid sent Delbert a disdainful look as if to say what could a paraplegic know about soccer.

"I'm rested. Let's go on," Sylvia coaxed.

Delbert moved on in a depressed mood. He hated when it swept over him. The answer was always to combat it with fresh challenges, projects which gave his high-powered brain grist to chew on.

## Chapter 8

Cynthia was in her mid teens when her parents separated and abandoned her to an uncle on Salt Spring Island. To say her departure from Campbell River was traumatic would be understatement. Ripped from a school environment in which she prospered and enjoyed popularity, only to be subjected to a life of drug addiction at the hands of her uncle, she now approached the town with trepidation. Would she run into either birth parent? She could only view them with deep resentment and none of the forgiveness Sylvia encouraged her to show.

When she left, her mother worked as a waitress in the Beehive Cafe. To avoid it, Cynthia turned up the hill to the hospital. She wanted to see her future work area and meet the administrator. That proved worthwhile since he gave her a tour of the hospital and some good advice on where to find an apartment.

Late in the afternoon, she located a furnished unit that not only had a great view over the ocean but also rented for a price she could afford on her intern salary. Thanks to Delbert and Sylvia, she had enough in the bank to pay earnest money and carry her over until her first paycheck. For the millionth time, she sent a mental thank you to them. They were now her real parents, regardless of legalities.

It didn't take long to move her meager carload of stuff into the apartment. Arms full with her last load, a young man came up the sidewalk behind her.

"Let me get that door for you."

"Thank you."

He held the door to let her pass, a warm smile lit up his handsome face. *Looks aren't everything,* she thought, *but they are a nice ingredient.* He seemed slightly bashful in a way that put her at ease.

"Do you live in this apartment?"

"Yes, on the second floor. John Carson."

"Cynthia Adams. I'll be on the third floor."

"Can I help with your things?"

"No. This is the last load. Thanks. Nice to meet you."

"You too."

She began to think Campbell River might have more to offer than a good professional internship as she unpacked and stowed belongings. *John Carson is an easy name to remember, thanks to Johnny Carson. He doesn't seem like the comedian type. I hope he has a sense of humour at least. Thia, back off. For all you know, he's locked into some woman already and you can't make a ten second judgement. Well, as Dad says, maybe you can. I wonder if he did. Oh, stop it.*

She decided to eat dinner at Rosie's café, the only Chinese restaurant in town. It was a favorite before she left. Always a pleasure to chat with the little old man who owned it. She hoped he was still alive.

"Hey Missy. Where you been? No see you long time."

"Hi Rosie, Yes, I've been gone."

"Missy all grown up now. Very pretty. Boys after you I bet."

She laughed, "Some. Do you still have your famous dry pork spareribs?"

"Oh, sure. You want?"

"Please."

"I fix special one for you. Welcome back kind. You like."

"I know I will Rosie. You make me glad to be here."

When he brought the meal, she hesitantly asked a question he could probably answer. People often failed to appreciate his grasp of English and powers of observation.

"Do you happen to know if my mother still works at the Beehive?"

A look of surprise and sadness crossed his face. "You not talk to your mother?"

"No. Between you and me, my parents abandoned me when they split up. I haven't seen them since."

"That bad. How they do that to you?" He shook his head. "Yes, she still there. Live with other man now."

"Please don't tell anyone I'm back. I need to think things out before I run into her. I have a new family now."

"Okay Missy. I keep secret."

Off and on throughout the evening, her thoughts ran to her birth mother. She worked hard to temper the anger she felt. Probably her birth father was more to blame. When he deserted them, he left Mary with more than she could support on a waitress salary. And it wasn't fair to think she should have known Luke was so evil. What would she have done in Mary's place? She would have found a way, some way, to keep her daughter. The resentment returned.

It looked like she faced a fitful night. *Better to think again about the comedian. Not a comedian, silly. Think of him as he is, an attractive man. His eyes were so blue, I could swim in them. How would it feel to be held by him, to dance, to kiss--*she drifted off to sleep with the semblance of a smile that reflected her resilient spirit?

# Chapter 9

After two weeks of heavy work, the crew was ready for three days off in town. Joe got Ned aside after dinner.

"Remember, we can't be seen together in town."

"Geez, Joe. How long do we have to go on with this? Don't you think it's blown over?"

Joe's eyes bore into him. "It's only been a few weeks and we don't know if the punk bit it or not."

"Wish you wouldn't talk that way. He was just a kid minding his own business until we showed up."

Joe's eyes never left him. Never blinked. It reminded Ned of a snake.

"Remember, Ned, you're in this as deep as I am. If he's dead, you're an accomplice to murder."

"I know. I know."

"What are you doing this weekend?"

"Think I'll go down to Courtenay. See if I can find some action there. How about you?"

"I'm going to shack up with Mabel." A sense of unfairness mixed with envy welled up in Ned.

\* \* \*

Ned pretended to have something to do at the last moment so they would have separate flights into town. He didn't want to spend the money on a taxi to Courtenay and since Joe had commandeered their car, he trudged over to the bus station. Like so many times before, he felt used. *Joe didn't need the car this weekend.*

Oblivious to Ned's needs, Joe arrived at Mabel's house just as a tall man came out. Mabel seemed cool, even tense when Joe entered.

"Who was that?"

"A new Mountie in town." She seemed nervous.

"What did he want?"

She confessed, "We dated once."

Joe's voice hardened. "What?"

"You don't have exclusive rights to my time, Joe."

"Bitch! Screwing around behind my back."

He slapped her hard. She screamed. He slammed her back against the wall. She slid to the floor. Joe felt himself grabbed from behind and thrown out the door. The Mountie bent over Mabel.

"Are you okay?"

"Yes—watch out Jack!"

The warning came too late. Joe rabbit punched him and tried to apply a choke hold. Jack twisted to parry it. He blocked a wild swing from Joe and hit him hard on the jaw. Joe staggered backward. Jack was over him in a flash, a knee on each arm and a tight grip on his throat.

"If I was in uniform, you'd be on your way to jail with an assault charge. But I'm not and we have ways of handling pricks like you that don't waste court time. I'll give you one chance to clear out and never come near Mabel again. There won't be a second chance. Understand?"

Joe said nothing. Just a cold evil stare. Jack raised his head and banged it hard on the sidewalk.

"Understand?"

Joe rasped out an okay. Jack stood up and let Joe turn over and rise on his knees, then stand up. He turned to face the man a foot taller than him with a physique that intimidated even him. He pushed his anger down inside, flashed a nasty glance at Mabel and turned away. They watched him peel rubber as he sped off.

"Are you sure you're okay?"

"I'll be fine. I'm sorry I got you involved in this."

"Don't be. Who is he?"

"Joe Carson. He works up in a logging camp."

"He's a mean character. How did you get mixed up with him?"

Tears formed in her eyes. "I started to date him a couple of years ago. He seemed macho and I was younger and more foolish. Then I couldn't break it off. Once he found out I had dated another guy. He beat him up so bad he was in the hospital for a week. I was afraid to date anyone else."

She sobbed now. He drew her to him to comfort her.

"I thought it would be safe with you. Now I don't know."

"You are safe with me. Mean as he is, he knows better than to mess with the law. But we need to make sure he leaves you alone. I'm going to reinforce that. "

"Be careful, Jack, please."

"Don't worry. That's my job."

She felt safe in his arms, but an undercurrent of apprehension remained.

\* \* \*

When Joe had left Mabel and Jack on Friday night, he drove around town in a blind rage for twenty minutes. Each time he headed back toward them, the thought of attacking the Mountie forced him away. Eventually he gave up and drove to the Quinsam Hotel. After registering, he headed into the beer parlour. Within an hour, he had picked a fight which turned into a brawl when one of his opponent's pals came to his rescue. No one helped Joe. They left him dazed on the sidewalk, blood oozing from his nose.

On Saturday morning, he cleaned up and drove into town for breakfast at the Beehive Café. Those who knew him took one look at the bruised jaw and black eye, then looked away, secretly pleased. As he headed back out of town, a short siren burst and flashing red light pulled him over. He rolled down the window as Jack approached.

"Why the hell did you stop me?"

"Just want to make sure you take my warning seriously. Stay away from Mabel or that bashed up face you're sporting will be the least of your problems."

"You can have that bitch for all I care."

"This is the last time I'll let you insult her too."

Joe started to say something, then thought better of it and sat silent. After staring at him for a moment, Jack walked back to his car, turned off the flashing light and drove away. Joe shook with helpless rage for long minutes. Finally, he gave up, drove to the seaplane dock and caught the next flight back to camp.

Ned had a somewhat better weekend in Courtenay. He picked up a girl in a bar Saturday night who agreed to spend the night with him. However, who picked up whom became questionable when she insisted on a donation to help support her two-year old child. Still, it proved to be a satisfying investment. He arrived back in camp on Sunday evening in much better spirits than Joe.

At breakfast in the mess tent, one of the burly loggers looked at Joe and laughed. "Ned, what happened to your wife? You beat her up?"

Joe started to lunge at the man. Ned grabbed him and dragged him back down.

"You might want to think twice about insulting Joe, Harry. And insulting me too."

"Take it easy, Ned. I didn't mean to insult you."

"We aren't a couple, Harry."

"Okay, okay, I was just kidding. Didn't mean to offend either of you."

Ned let it go. Joe's stare caused Harry's hair to bristle. He felt an involuntary shiver and a premonition that it was far from over in Joe's mind. He decided he better keep an eye on Joe in future.

# Chapter 10

"So, when are you females going to turn us males into worker drones like a bee colony."

"That's kind of a snide comment. You obviously don't think much of what Virginia said."

"Actually, I agree with everything you said. Yesterday, I did a little research in the library. There's a lot of data that supports your theory."

"Virginia's information."

"Right. Anyway, over a century ago there was a French child born with both male and female genitals. At first, they treated her as a girl and called her Alexina. But when she reached puberty, instead of growing breasts and having a period, she grew facial hair. Still living as a girl, she fell in love with a series of girls through her twenties. Eventually, doctors dictated that she be considered a male and she/he then became Abel. This ruined her love life and she committed suicide at thirty-four. The male hormones apparently took precedence although she was comfortable living in a sexual limbo."

"Very interesting but what's that got to do with the rest of us?"

"By studying people like her who are not fully developed males or females, one can conclude that the sex is not completely determined when the egg is fertilized. It emerges as the embryo develops. In fact, you might say right up through puberty. That supports the theory all embryos start out female and roughly half of them are converted to male as they grow. Kind of a hard pill for our male egos to swallow."

"Poor dears."

"What interests me more is how male and female brains and operating styles develop. They are subject to this hormone influence just like the conspicuous physical attributes. You females have it all over us there."

"Now I'm really listening."

"Your brains are wired to cooperate with others and work together to find solutions, you are less emotional believe it or not, and you handle stress better resulting in typically longer lives. And that's despite the burden of reproduction of our species."

"I wish the world's leaders and politicians could hear that and be convinced it's true."

"Yes. And it seems realistic to extrapolate the theory to suggest that disruption of this hormonal morphing from female to male may prevent many individuals from becoming heterosexual or leave them gender confused."

"That's an interesting perspective. Hate to turn away from this lofty topic but I got word today they want me to transition to the upper island assignment on August first."

"We better start a house search in Campbell River. I'll notify Vic College that I won't be back in the Fall."

"Are you sure you want to do that?"

"I'm ready to move on. If it takes a while to get established up island, I can fly you to work from here at first."

"My own special air taxi. Course you provide that service already."

"Since Campbell River is sort of a medical care center for the north half of the island and on up the coast, I think Delboat would make a good medical evacuation plane."

"You'd have to accommodate a stretcher."

"We could do that with a few modifications. I've mulled over some design changes that would give us room for a stretcher behind me and we could add a post to hold an IV bag. It might reduce the baggage space on your side but we hardly ever use that anyway."

"Are you looking for more excuses to fly?"

"More ways to be useful. Think I'll call Tony to see if he wants to do the work."

* * *

Tony arrived at the dock on Sunday.

"What're you up to now, Delbert?"

"I want to equip her with a stretcher behind me."

Tony lowered the door to its ramp position and started taking measurements.

"Looks like the issue will be loading the stretcher in with a patient on it. How wide would it have to be?"

"Twenty inches, at least eighteen."

"Where would you store it?"

"It would have to fold up and get locked on the floor behind the door so I can get in and out."

Tony scratched his head and took more measurements as he visualized how it would work.

"Guess it would have to lock to the floor when you are carrying a patient as well. Should it be mounted on springs to counter your rough landings?"

Delbert laughed. "That would be a bonus. Also, there needs to be a vertical post with a bracket to hold an IV."

"Sure you don't want OR lighting as well?"

They both laughed this time. Tony made a sketch of the layout and marked a few dimensions on it.

"Okay, let me work on this and get back to you."

\* \* \*

He called back on Tuesday morning.

"I can get an eighty-inch long, twenty-inch wide stretcher in but it has to be narrower at the foot end. When the head and foot ends fold over the center section, it fits in the space behind the door except for one inch. How far apart are the wheels on your wheelchair?"

"About twenty inches. Why?"

"You need to roll over the floor brackets that it will lock into. I can keep them to a fifteen-inch span."

"That's no problem. What will it cost?"

"Think of it as my contribution to Island health care. Do you want me to go ahead with it?"

"We'll call it Tony's bed."

\* \* \*

It took only a week for Tony to make the stretcher despite a busy workload in his bicycle shop. He loved to create custom equipment and had to admit some routine jobs were pushed aside. He called to say he would be out with it on Sunday. They agreed to meet on the dock again.

* * *

Delbert marvelled at the artistry. The head and foot pieces automatically locked when unfolded. The center section sat on four springs over a four-legged frame that would latch to the floor in either the stowed or carry position. A patient's ride would be further cushioned by a latticework of straps hung from the upper frame.

"That's elegantly functional, Tony. Patients will ride in more comfort than we do. It's fantastic!"

Tony smiled. "Let's locate it where you want and I'll install the mounting brackets."

The coup de grâce occurred when Tony brought out a chrome post with an IV hook and snapped it onto the stretcher.

"Thought it would be better to attach it to the stretcher than the airplane so it can travel with the victim."

"Sylvia will be thrilled with this."

"I hope so. Did you think I was trying to please you?"

"Guess not. Show me how it stows."

As Tony had claimed, it protruded into the door opening less than an inch. After admiring it a little longer, Delbert locked up the plane.

"You put a lot into this. Let me pay you something for it."

"No."

"Well, the least I can do is have Sylvia ask the Public Health Department to issue a donation receipt to give you an income tax deduction."

"I'll accept that if it's easily done."

* * *

Delbert flew Sylvia to Port Renfrew on Tuesday. She doted over the new stretcher and insisted on setting it up, then stowing it again.

"I need to know how it works. Tony did a great job."

"He'll appreciate hearing that from you."

After dropping Sylvia off, Delbert had two hours to kill. He flew on up the coast and into Port Alberni, then turned south through the mountains.

Before he realized where he was, he recognized the mountain pass where Chuck Lansbury had collided with him. In his mind, he lived again the flight that ultimately cost him his feet and the use of his legs. He visualized the fighter cockpit, remembered how Chuck flew up his back, how he was too close to the ground to push the nose down. He yelled over the radio for Chuck to pull up. When he was finally free, it took only a moment to realize Chuck's afterburners had destroyed his vertical fin and rudder.

He didn't want to dwell on the flight down to Royal Colwood Golf Course with hydraulics failing and almost no control left. He tried to not think of the rock jutting out of the fairway but of course that just drew his attention to it. Not that big a rock—just enough to veer him off course and into the cliff. His memory stopped there. He turned west to Port Renfrew with a desolate feeling worse than anything he had experienced in years.

When Sylvia showed up at the dock, she sensed his mood immediately. "What's the matter, dear?"

"Nothing." He knew she wouldn't buy that. "Well, I inadvertently found myself flying through the pass where we collided. The memories came flooding back."

She gently stroked the back of his wrist. "It's often hard to live with the adversity life brings us."

That reminded him of what she had survived and forced him back to the present. "It brought us together again. That makes up for everything." He tried a smile and found it genuine. The melancholy spell was broken.

Later, on the flight home, Sylvia mentioned, "I've made a lot of friends on this end of the island. I'm going to miss them. There was a little old woman back there who has no one to talk to except me. It brightens her day when we show up. Made it hard to tell her someone else would be coming in future. We both had tears in our eyes."

"You are the ultimate empath, honey. There will be a lot of lonely little old ladies up island that will latch onto you."

"Don't make it sound like a burden. I enjoy helping them."

"As a matter of fact, you may still see her. Port Renfrew could as easily be covered from up island as Victoria."

## Chapter 11

Almost a week passed without Cynthia running into her mother. She knew it was only a matter of time. Still, she could not predict how either of them would react. She repeatedly composed little speeches for the occasion only to discard them later as either ludicrous or inadequate. They would just have to let the event unfold when it happened.

The week had borne fruit professionally. Following a senior doctor on his hospital rounds, she liked his bedside manner, a mixture of compassion and cheerfulness that left patients in better spirits when he moved on. He insisted she read each chart and often asked her opinion. She knew he measured her abilities, but she never felt threatened, only grateful for the experience he imparted.

Quiet evenings in her apartment inevitably brought her thoughts back to Mary. She refrained from exposure in town out of fear of meeting Mary. *This is ridiculous. I need to go down to the café and confront her once and for all.* Not yet committed to it, she procrastinated another day. On Thursday, she moved to night shift so the afternoon presented an opportunity she could not ignore.

She drove quickly to the Beehive Café and walked in before the urge to bolt overwhelmed her. *Perhaps she won't be working.* But she was. Cynthia sat down at a table for two and watched her deal with another customer. Then she turned toward Cynthia, took two steps, stopped, stared, came slowly forward.

"Cynthia?"

"Yes, Mary. I'm back in town."

"How come? You look good, all grown up."

"Thank you. I'm a doctor now—an intern at the hospital for a year at least."

"A doctor—you're a doctor?"

"Yes, Mary."

"I'm your mother. Why are you calling me Mary?"

"That's your name. I'm afraid I don't consider you my mother now."

Confused, "Did Luke put you through medical school?"

"Luke's dead. He turned me into a drug addicted prostitute."

Mary gasped. "I—I didn't know. How awful! But I heard he was killed in a drug raid…how did you become a doctor after that?"

"My new parents saved me and sent me to college."

"New parents?"

"Yes. They live in Victoria."

Mary seemed completely lost. "But I'm your mother…"

"Not anymore."

The air was emotionally charged. Cynthia felt her heart beating wildly. Mary struggled to make sense out of their conversation.

"Luke and your father were no good. He used to beat me, you know."

"I don't remember that."

"When you were young. The Mounties made him stop."

"Where is he now?"

"Last I heard he was up in Port Hardy. Stay away from him, Cynthia."

"I never want to see him again."

Slowly, things fell into place for Mary, "You must make a lot of money as a doctor?"

"Not as an intern."

"But you will when you start a practice?"

"Perhaps."

"Life has been very hard for me on a waitress salary."

"You're living with a new man."

"How did you know?"

"It's common knowledge in town."

Mary became defensive. "Did you expect me to go on struggling alone in hopes your father came back?"

"No. It's your life. I don't care what you do."

"You will abandon me just like your father did," she whimpered.

"He's not my father and I will abandon you just like you abandoned me."

Cynthia stood and walked out. Mary watched her go. Back in her car, Cynthia sat behind the wheel and cried. Cried because she knew it would hurt her birth mother. Cried because she deserved to be hurt. Cried because she knew Sylvia would be disappointed in her unforgiving nature. Cried because that didn't matter as much as the unforgivable act of sending her into Luke's clutches. Cried because she made no effort to contact her when she heard Luke was killed. Long minutes passed before she regained sufficient composure to drive home.

Night shift kept her busy. Yet, in the quiet moments her mind returned to the earlier encounter. Had it really settled things? What about the next time their paths crossed? Could she simply not acknowledge her presence? That was not her nature. She realized she must somehow find a way to be civil while cool and strong to resist attempts Mary might make to regain mother status. *It took less than two minutes for her to start angling for money!*

At times, she wished she had taken her internship in some other city. But realistically, the need to reconcile her feelings toward both birth parents would exist no matter where she went. Better to face it head on, just like she did with the stain of addiction. Her thoughts turned to Delbert and Sylvia. She wished they were here already. They always bolstered her confidence, two pillars to lean on. Her true parents.

# Chapter 12

In mid July, Delbert and Sylvia flew to Campbell River to spend a weekend in search of a house. Cynthia found time to do some research on their behalf. She had half a dozen possibilities lined up. There would be no mention of her encounter with Mary. She didn't want to burden them. A happy feeling welled up as she watched Delboat slip into the dock, Sylvia waving from the right seat. As usual, Delbert docked on her side first, then turned the plane around to tie up on his side.

"Hi Thia. Hope you haven't waited long?"

"Hi Mum. Only about five minutes. Dad's ETA was accurate as usual."

They tied the mooring lines as Delbert shut down everything and rolled out.

"Hi Dad." She bent over to give him a brief hug. "I found a few house possibilities for you. Afraid it's not easy to find single-level houses."

"That's not surprising with so much sloping terrain."

The ramp up from the dock was barely wide enough for a wheelchair but that was no obstacle compared to the gravel parking lot.

"I need mountain bike wheels on this rig."

"Wait here. I'll bring the car over."

It was one more of the minor frustrations Delbert felt when he had to rely on others. Once they were all in the car and the wheelchair folded in the trunk, Cynthia set off for town.

"I have lunch fixings back at the apartment. We have time to look at a couple of places first if you like?"

"Sure."

The first two houses were on level ground above the hill leading into town. Neither appealed to them, both a little the worse for wear and in need of paint. One had a strong smell of poorly accommodated pets. In proven real estate sales strategy, Cynthia saved the best for last. They drove back to her apartment with both parents slightly discouraged.

"This is an attractive place. I love your view out over the water."

"It's a shame to live in Campbell River without a view."

"I have two houses with views to show you after lunch."

\* \* \*

The first house, on South Murphy Street, had a slightly restricted view of the ocean and close in looked down on a marina. It was not a large house but it appeared workable for Delbert, definitely a possibility.

The second house was further south on Ridgeview Place. It provided a full panoramic view of the ocean with Quadra Island across the channel and distant snow-capped mountains beyond. They found the interior attractive and loved the setting.

The main floor was at street level. Lawn sloped down on either side of the house and allowed for a daylight basement on the water side. Delbert would not be able to negotiate the inside stairs, but he could handle the sidewalk along side the house. At the foot of the lawn, a fairly steep drop-off to the highway level below was not protected with either a fence or railing. That surprised them but they figured the owner wanted an unobstructed view. Though priced to sell, it was expensive.

"We could live in the last one, however, it doesn't match this place. The large double garage here would be great for any project I might take on and the view is exceptional."

Sylvia could tell how the search would end. "Thia, are any of the others you found up to the standard of these two?"

"Not really," she confessed.

"Can we afford this one, dear?"

"Once we sell the house in Victoria we can."

"Then, let's make an offer with that contingency, assuming you're okay with wheeling up and down the sidewalk?"

"I can manage that. We might look into one of those stair climbers though."

Minds made up, they approached the owner, who had elected not to go with a real estate agent, explained the need for a contingency and made an offer ten thousand below his list price.

"Do you have financing available?"

"It will be a cash deal."

"How long do you need to sell your house?"

"Let's shoot for thirty days and review the situation again if that doesn't work out."

"Okay, I'll have my lawyer draw up a contract. Can you put up five thousand earnest money?"

"Certainly." They shook hands and exchanged phone numbers. Cynthia added hers and offered to bridge the gap between them.

On the way back to the apartment, Sylvia broke the silence. "Did you look over the edge of that embankment?"

Cynthia did. Delbert stayed clear of it. Sylvia continued, "It's a long way down. You'll have to be careful, dear."

Delbert laughed, "You think I will roll off the edge."

"Or get pushed off," she responded with a chuckle.

# Chapter 13

With her chosen parents on their way back to Victoria, Cynthia returned home a little melancholy. John drove up behind her. They entered the apartment together.

He opened the conversation. "Hi Cynthia. I've been hoping our paths would cross again."

She laughed, "You didn't have to wait for a chance meeting."

He gave her a sheepish smile. "I didn't want to seem too forward. Would you like to join me for a drink to get better acquainted?"

"If you have something non-alcoholic I would."

"Sure, I've got a few kinds of pop or tea if you prefer."

She followed him into his apartment and marveled at how meticulous it looked. *I better clean up my mess before he sees it.* A model float plane on the sideboard caught her eye.

"You like airplanes?"

"That's a Beaver, workhorse of the north. I'm a pilot. Fly for Van Isle Airlines. Would you like a coke, ginger ale, seven-up or tea?"

"Ginger ale would be nice. I'm a pilot too. At least, I have a private license."

"A flying doctor. You're very talented."

"How did you know I'm a doctor?"

"The apartment manager told me."

"A flying detective. What else did he tell you?"

They both laughed. "That's all he knew about you."

"What could he tell me about you?"

"Not much, hopefully." He passed her the glass.

"Why? What dark secrets are you hiding?

He paused. She sensed a sudden reluctance. "Well, I guess he might tell you my father abandoned us just before my brother and I turned teenagers."

She stared at him in shock. He continued sadly, "He might also tell you we had a stream of strange men visiting for years while she raised us."

She responded in a quiet voice. "I can relate to some of that. My parents abandoned me when I was in Grade eleven."

It was his turn to look shocked. "Both abandoned you?"

"Yes, they sent me to live with an uncle."

"Well, at least you had that. Did he put you through medical school?"

"No. He turned me into a drug addict."

"What? Are you pulling my leg?"

"No. I've found it's best to get everything out up front so you might as well hear the whole thing. I was a drug addicted prostitute for about half a year before my current parents rescued me. They put me through medical school."

She noted a strange look on his face, almost an angry look. *I've lost him on our first date.* Gradually his features softened.

"That's terrible."

"It's in the past. I've been addiction-free for eight years now. Still, I don't take chances. That's why I steer clear of alcohol."

"Strange. We have two serious things in common. One good, one bad."

"Can we bury the bad one?"

"Yes. That's what we should do." He smiled but his body language was slightly disconcerting.

"Where's your brother now?"

"He works in a logging camp up the coast. We seldom see each other. Don't really have anything in common."

*You were both abandoned by your father and raised by your mother who was a hooker. Is that what my mother would have had to do?*

Time to change subjects. "Tell me about your flying."

"Growing up I always wanted to be a pilot. Used to hang around the seaplane dock in Comox doing any job they let me. Eventually they hired me for next to starvation wages, which was okay because the pilots sometimes took me along when ferrying cargo with no passengers. I pestered them into teaching me to fly, navigate, the works."

"That wouldn't get you a license."

"No. But when they realized I had become a good pilot, they started logging my hours and sponsored me right through to a commercial license. Then, they paid me regular pilot pay and here I am."

"You showed a lot of initiative and perseverance. That's admirable."

"Thank you. I won't deny it was a long struggle."

"Sort of like medical school."

"Guess we have three things in common," he laughed.

"Right. On that note, I should get going. Thanks for the drink. It seems like we've learned an awful lot about each other in a remarkably short time."

"Can I still knock on your door sometime?"

"Please do." Again, something in his body language flitted through her subconscious and left her mildly disconcerted.

# Chapter 14

The Victoria house sold after four days on the market. Delbert naturally assumed they had asked too little. Sylvia reminded him they got what they wanted. It was more than enough to cover the Campbell River house. He knew better than to argue with her logic. They called Cynthia and asked her to let the seller know they could close now.

Two hours later, she called back. "He said fine. You can move in as soon as you like. He asks that you transfer the money to his bank here."

"Our bank will open an account in their Campbell River branch and transfer our money to it. We'll move it to his account when we sign the closing papers."

"That's the way to go. I'll tell him."

Within a day, they arranged for a moving company to handle everything. All Sylvia did was pack the things she wanted to take in the car. Delbert would fly the airplane up island. Things came together at lightening pace and a week later they were stashing belongings away in the new house. Cynthia helped as time permitted.

On the second afternoon, Delbert barbecued salmon and sweet potato sprinkled with cinnamon while the women worked. He wheeled back and forth between grill and kitchen. The result displayed on the table included green beans with bacon bits and an attractive salad.

"What a masterpiece, Dad!"

"Least I could do while you two slaved."

"Have you got permanent moorage for Delboat?"

"They're renting me a spot on the seaplane docks in the river, near the ramp to make it easier for me to navigate the wheelchair. They kidded me saying they wanted Delboat close to the ramp so they wouldn't have gawkers down on the floats."

"It still catches people's eye."

"They want to stick with their preconceived view of what an airplane should look like and fail to consider the role function plays in design."

Sylvia changed the subject. "How do you like your job, Thia?"

"It's great. Doctor Munson is an excellent role model. I'm learning a lot from him. He has a wonderful way with patients."

"Good. Are you meeting other friends too?"

"Are you worried about my social life?"

"Worried? No. Just curious," she laughed. "Have you met any of your school year acquaintances?"

A slight frown slipped across Cynthia's face. "Not yet."

"That seems to bother you."

"How do you manage to read minds?"

"Not minds. Body language," Delbert interjected.

"Well, if you must know, I ran into my birth mother the other day. Not an enjoyable experience."

"How is she?"

"Okay, I guess. She still works as a waitress at the Beehive Café. She now lives with another man."

Sylvia fought down a jealous feeling. In her mind, the birth mother took precedence over any other caregiver.

"Well, now you can resurrect your relationship with her."

"I have no intention of doing that. In fact, I will avoid contact with her as much as possible."

"Cynthia! That's not right."

"I will remain abandoned." Her tone indicated the subject was closed. "On the bright side, there's an attractive young pilot living in our building who I hope to build a friendship with."

"That's nice. You have flying in common." Sylvia filed away the need to approach Cynthia gingerly regarding her mother. It bothered her to realize she secretly wanted to be first in Cynthia's heart.

"When do you start your new job, Mum?"

"Tomorrow, I suppose. On Tuesday, Delbert will fly me into the village at Tahsis for the first time."

\* \* \*

Later, as Cynthia rested in her apartment before her nightshift, John came knocking, as promised.

"Got a moment to talk?"

"Sure, come in. I have half an hour before my shift starts."

"Thanks. I'll come right to the point. I have a small cabin on a beautiful inland lake. It's a peaceful place to commune with nature, fish, hike, explore or simply relax with a great view. I'm off next weekend. How would you like to fly in and see it Saturday morning? We could overnight and come back Sunday afternoon. No strings attached. Just relaxation."

"You make it sound idyllic."

"It really is."

She hesitated. It seemed a little early in their relationship to be running off overnight. *That's silly. We're both responsible adults and it looks like a good way to get to know each other better.*

"As it stands right now, I have the weekend off too. I'd like to go with you, but you should be aware they can call me in even at the last moment."

"I'll take my chances with that. Let's plan to set off at nine Saturday morning."

"What can I bring?"

"If you want, lunch for us that day. I will have food for the other meals—and beverages, including ginger ale," he added with a laugh.

"I look forward to it."

"Me too. Better let you get ready for work."

It struck her a bit strange how he left as soon as the date was settled but she attributed it to a streak of shyness or perhaps it really was consideration for her time.

# Chapter 15

Tuesday morning Sylvia rechecked the contents of her nurse's kit. In addition to first aid supplies, there was an assortment of inoculation and vaccination paraphernalia. Her job was more preventative in nature than treatment. There could be cuts and rashes to treat. Beyond that, she looked out for more serious wounds, infections and sicknesses that called for medical attention, perhaps even hospitalization. Delbert's medivac capability made possible flying a serious case out on their return trip.

Within an hour, Delbert taxied out into the river in search of a clear takeoff run. Delboat's quietness was a drawback now. Boaters could hear the other seaplanes takeoff roar and steer clear. They would not hear him coming so he made sure there was nothing heading into his lane. On the other hand, he became airborne in a much shorter distance than the other planes and so within minutes he climbed out of the river mouth and headed west.

"How long do you think you need in the village?"

"Hard to tell. Let's plan on four hours."

"Okay, once you're established with the locals, I'll fly around the coast in that vicinity, do a little sightseeing. If I find a good fishing spot, I may set down and try my luck."

"Fine."

\* \* \*

A floating dock at Tahsis provided a place to let Sylvia off. Delbert watched her trudge up the dirt road, toting her heavy kit. *She loves to help people.* As usual, he felt again his admiration and love for her.

Tahsis was primarily a tribal fishing village although the intrusion of logging now hired many of the men. It had a small building near the dock that looked like a store. Sylvia made for that. An old man greeted her inside.

"Good morning. My name is Sylvia Pillage. I'm the new public health nurse in this region. Can you tell me who the village leader is and where I might find him or her?"

"Him. Joseph Longneck. Second house on the right."

"Thank you."

He grunted, "Hope you're better than the last one. Hardly ever showed and never did much to help our sick."

"I certainly hope to do better."

He turned back to the magazine in front of him.

Sylvia carried on up to the second house and knocked on the door. Minutes passed before it opened to reveal a tall, elderly man. She noted with slight amusement that he did in fact have a long neck.

"Yes?"

She explained her role again and asked if there was an empty room in the village that she could use to administer to anyone in need.

"There's a community meeting room in that building across the road." She followed his pointing finger.

"Is there a way you can spread word that I'm here if anyone needs medical attention?"

He looked sceptical. "Suppose we can get one of the kids to go around knocking on doors. We got one damn serious problem but you can't help with it."

"Oh. What's that?"

"James Wakium has gone off his rocker. Got his wife and kids locked up in his shack and threatening to shoot anyone who comes near."

"How long has he been there?"

"This is the fourth day. I just found out about it this morning. Called the Mounties in Campbell River but who knows when they will find time to get here?"

"Have they got food and water?"

"Doubt it. He's been out of work for a while. They carry water in from a well so he's not letting them out to do that either."

"Hasn't anyone tried to talk him out?"

"I shouted to him this morning and he sent a bullet that almost parted my hair."

"How old are the children?"

"About five, three and a baby born in the Spring."

"They can't last long without water. We need to get them out. Where's his place?"

"Just over the crest of the hill but don't you go near. He's crazy enough to shoot you."

Sylvia carried her kit across the road and left it in the meeting room, then headed up the hill. Joseph watched her. She won't actually go near him once she sees the layout. Still, he had misgivings. It was always hard to figure out the ways of strangers. A few others noticed her climbing the hill. Curiosity led to speculation that sped from house to house. By the time she reached the top, a group of spectators had gathered part way down the hill behind her.

Sylvia stood on the crest with the rising sun behind her and called out.

"James. Come out. I want to talk to you. I will protect you and keep you safe. Come out now."

Inside, James raised his rifle and peered over the open windowsill. He could barely make out a woman dressed all in white with golden hair glistening in the sun. He raised the gun and fired over her head.

"James. I am not moving until you come out. Put down your gun and come to me. I will ease your mind and fix your troubles. Come to me."

Her voice was melodic, calm, almost hypnotic. He stared at her shimmering on the crest and wondered if he was hallucinating. *Who is she? Is she the Virgin Mary? She must be. Has she come to save us?*

Sylvia could see his head in the window. "Come, James."

Slowly, he moved to the door and cracked it open. There was no one else on this side of the hill. *She must be alone. She must be Our Mother.* He moved outside, the gun hanging at his side. He trembled.

"Put the gun down and come here James."

He dropped the gun and staggered toward her. *She is so beautiful.* "Mother, forgive me." He fell to his knees in front of her. Sylvia realized his confusion and decided to continue the illusion.

"Why have you kept your family captive?"

"I cannot provide for them."

"But others can help."

"No, Mother. They let us starve to death."

She looked back down the hill at a crowd now assembled to witness the spectacle. A man approached carrying a rifle. She held up her hand to stop him and waved him back.

"James, I will see that you and your family are fed. Do you trust me?"

"Yes, Mother."

"Go and bring your family to me."

He turned back to the shack and soon led out his wife with the baby in her arms, followed by two emaciated children. They were all weak, hardly able to stagger up to her. She turned with them beside her and faced the crowd below and raised her voice.

"These are your people, your family. How can you abandon them in their hour of need? Any of you might be here in their place."

Many heads hung down. Some feet scuffed the dirt. One woman spoke up. "We didn't know until it was too late."

"In a small community, we must all look out for each other. We must watch for signs of trouble and rush to fix any problem that arises."

There were murmurs of assent and remorse.

"Please organize people amongst you to bring food and water to the Wakium house. We need to make tea with lots of sugar and soup. Then move on to solid food later."

People started to scurry, some to their houses, other up the hill to help the family back to their house and fetch water. Sylvia moved back with the family, who were all still in shock. She made them sip the water first and warned them not to gulp it down. The baby appeared barely alive. Its mother obviously could not nurse it.

She asked the helpers, "Is there some one in the village nursing now?"

A woman nodded and sent her boy off to get the nursing mother. James' wife was crying. Sylvia passed the baby to another woman and hugged the distraught mother. James had tears running down his face too. The two children clung to his legs. He stroked their heads absentmindedly.

When the nursing mother arrived, she took the baby and encouraged it to suck her life-giving milk. She was a big woman. Sylvia thought she would have no problem nursing a second child. James' wife looked on with envy. People began to show up with food. Sylvia organized them to begin with tea laced with sugar while they built a fire and heated soup. Others began to clean the shack. It looked as if the community had rallied to help the Wakiums.

Sylvia stepped back to let them take over. James stared at her. "I thought you were our Holy Mother."

"I apologize for letting you think that. It seemed to help you come out."

"You are our savior."

"The village will be your savior and some day your turn will come to save someone else in trouble."

James' wife calmed down and gratefully accepted the nourishment offered. Sylvia spoke a little louder to the group.

"You're doing a fine job. I'm leaving the care of the Wakiums in your hands. If any of you or others in the village want me to check your health, I'll be in the meeting room for a couple of hours."

She left amid a chorus of thank you and blessings which embarrassed her. There was an audible buzz as she walked over the crest of the hill. Alone back in the meeting room, she started to shake uncontrollably. *He could have shot me. No, he couldn't. Underneath the stress of his situation, he's a good man.* She wondered why a man in a desperate situation would choose death for himself and his family over begging for help. Was it simply pride? A destroyed self-image? The shaking passed.

She opened her kit on a table and sat down behind it to meditate.

# Chapter 16

Completely unaware of the crisis, Delbert flew out to Nootka Sound and circled Nootka Island. The rugged beauty of the west coast exposed to weather off the ocean amazed him. This was virgin wilderness except where logging left the land scarred. Such a shame to exploit and spoil this area.

He thought there would be salmon in the sound heading up the rivers to spawn. He made a note of where the fishing boats congregated and decided to not interfere with them. Over a promising stretch of water, he decided to land and fish for a while. He opened the window on his side, turned around and retrieved his rod and tackle. Soon he had a line in the water and moved along at a good trolling speed with the water jet.

For the next twenty minutes, there were no bites. That didn't bother him. Peace on the water cleansed his soul and let him contemplate a myriad of different things. Yet, when a fish finally struck, he appreciated the action. Landing a salmon in Delboat was not easy. He had to play it until sufficiently exhausted that it wouldn't bolt when he bounced it gently against the hull.

A fish up to ten pounds he could net and lift over the sill. For larger fish, he had to lower the ramp and haul them in back there. That was a touchy process in a wheelchair. If he went overboard, he didn't relish the idea of flailing his way back to the airplane and dragging himself up onto the ramp. If his wheelchair went in with him, it would be disastrous. He would have no way to fly the airplane. For that reason, he always tied a mooring line to the wheelchair when he fished alone.

This salmon looked to be about fifteen pounds. It was spent when he pulled it onto the ramp. He clubbed it to end its misery and prevent it from flopping around. Then cleaned it to prevent belly rot and splashed sea water on the ramp to get rid of the blood. It was time to go back and check on Sylvia.

* * *

Within fifteen minutes, a mother and child appeared in the meeting room doorway. Sylvia told them to come in and asked how she could help them. The little girl showed her a bad cut on her arm. The bleeding had been stopped but there were obvious signs of infection. The cut area was swollen and red. She noted telltale red streaks in her elbow.

"The cut is infected. I need to give you a penicillin shot to fight it. This will sting," she said as she wiped the cut with iodine. The girl flinched but remained stoic.

When Sylvia brought out the needle and filled it with the amount of penicillin appropriate for the girl's weight, her eyes widened. She moved closer to her mother.

"This won't hurt like the iodine did," Sylvia smiled. "I need to inject it into her posterior. The girl wore shorts. Sylvia turned her around, pulled her shorts down slightly and gave her the shot.

"That should fix her up. I want you to sit with her here for fifteen minutes. If the swelling and redness don't start to go away in three days, have Joseph Longneck call me."

"Thank you, Sister Sylvia."

Disconcerted, Sylvia asked, "Why did you call me that?"

"Chief Longneck said that's what we should call you. He thinks you are an angel sent to our aid in the village."

Sylvia shook her head and made a note to straighten out Joseph. Over the next hour, about a dozen adults and children came with a collection of cuts, rashes, aches and pains. One boy had broken the small bone in his lower leg without knowing it. She wrapped it with a splint to wear for three weeks.

"He really should see a doctor."

"There is no doctor here—ever."

"Do you trust me to take him back to Campbell River so a doctor can look at his leg? We will bring him back tomorrow or the next day."

"Yes Sister. I trust you."

"Bring him to the dock in an hour."

When the last visitor departed, Sylvia searched out Joseph Longneck.

"Apparently you told villagers I should be called Sister Sylvia. While it's true that I was once a nun, I'm just a simple nurse now."

"What you did means much more to us than that. You will always be highly respected in our village."

"Thank you. What did James do before this?"

"He fished but not very well. He lost his boat when he couldn't make payments."

"What else can he do?"

"He is good with his hands."

"Is there anything he could do that people would be willing to pay for."

Joseph paused, "I can't think of anything."

"I notice some houses have small gardens, not enough to provide vegetables year-round for everyone."

"We go without most of the time."

"Could James build a large community garden and grow things for everyone?"

Joseph thought for a minute. "Yes, I suppose he could."

He could see where she was headed and wondered if it would work. Would the village be willing to support the Wakiums until he got results?

"I'm not sure he knows how to grow things."

"My husband could show him how to build a garden and care for it."

*This woman has a will of iron. And perhaps she is right.*

"If I tell them you and your husband will help and if James is willing, the village will support building a garden. There is good soil for it where the river joins the sea."

Sylvia smiled warmly, "Thank you, Joseph—Chief Joseph."

He laughed as she headed out the door. Delbert's plane bobbed at the dock in the light chop. *I wonder how long he's waited there.* She picked up her kit and headed down. The woman with the boy stood near the dock, along with a growing group of onlookers. They chattered with each other, with frequent glances at the strange plane and wheelchair-bound man. They were suddenly quiet when Sylvia was spotted. A large boy ran to her and carried her kit down.

Sylvia took the limping boy's hand and led him onto the dock. "Hi, dear. We have a passenger to take back. He needs to have a doctor look at his leg."

"Fine. I'll turn the plane around so you two can get in."

Curiosity mounted as he wheeled onboard, raised the ramp and pulled away from the dock. When he brought it back in they realized he wasn't leaving without them. Sylvia raised the window, lowered the ramp on her side, helped the boy into the rear seat and buckled him in. As she raised the ramp from her front seat, the crowd waved. Many shouted, "Thank you, Sister Sylvia". She waved back and lowered the window.

Delbert turned to her as he taxied out. "Sister Sylvia?"

She laughed, "I'm not returning to the Sisterhood, if that's what you're wondering. I coaxed a man holed up with his family to come out and let people help him. They're grateful."

"He had a gun and shot at her," the boy piped up.

Sylvia needed to defuse the sharp look Delbert gave her. "He had no intention of harming me." Delbert was not appeased.

"Guess I shouldn't have left you alone," he muttered.

The boy was awestruck when the plane took off and silently soared into the sky. People at the dock stared with almost the same feeling. It was a day to remember and a story to relate for years to come.

# Chapter 17

Saturday morning arrived. Cynthia looked forward to a happy, relaxing weekend as she packed their lunch. She meant to let her parents know what she was up to but they were gone on Thursday taking the boy back to Tahsis sporting a cast on his leg. And on Friday they were off at another village. They hadn't returned last night. She assumed they had to stay a second day as Sylvia had expected.

John knocked precisely at nine. That didn't surprise her. *His meticulous attention to detail is a valuable quality in a pilot. Hope my apartment is neat enough to gain approval.*

He greeted her with a smile. "Ready?"

"Yes." She picked up her overnight bag and the chest with their lunch. Her things were stored beside a picnic chest in his trunk.

"Does the company let you use their seaplanes for this sort of thing?"

"No. I have a Cessna that I am gradually wrenching from the bank's clutches."

"I've only flown Delbert's flying boat. It will seem like we are a long way above the water in a float plane."

"That's the strangest looking flying boat I've ever seen."

She noticed he didn't offer to check her out in his plane. "It's cool to fly. So quiet. Very maneuverable and a real low stall speed. The main difference is the lack of rudder pedals. Rudder control is handled with a second joystick that also controls thrust."

"Sounds interesting. I'll have to ask Delbert to take me up for a spin sometime."

\* \* \*

John named a few lakes and mountains as they flew. Cynthia noted the bearing and when he circled their destination lake, she estimated they had flown about seventy-five miles. The lake was indeed remote. There had been no sign of habitation for miles. The pristine setting was beautiful, water lined by evergreen forest except for one small clearing that revealed the cabin with a small float in front.

"It's gorgeous!"

"Thought you'd like it. It's a great get-away place."

"How did you find it?"

"I didn't. My father found it and built the cabin before he deserted us. He was a pilot also. Flew a Beaver mostly. Used it to fly in building material. He brought us up here when we were small."

"And you never forgot it."

"It lay vacant for years. I've been fixing it up again."

"Do you ever bring your mother here?"

He looked at her sharply. "Not anymore. She disappeared two years ago."

"Disappeared?"

"We were on our own so she just took off one day."

"I'm sorry. I seem to always bring up difficult memories for you."

"That's okay. Nothing a relaxing weekend won't cure."

As they unloaded supplies, she noticed a small stream that emptied into the lake at the right edge of the clearing. It really was an idyllic spot. Across the lake, a forested hill fronted a snow-capped mountain range to the southeast. This would be a weekend to remember. She wondered if it would be the first of many.

After lunch, they took a short walk up the hill along the stream bed at first, then straight up to the peak. They could see for miles in every direction, over rolling, tree-covered hills. She found it breath-taking, like living in a different world. She told him so. He seemed to enjoy her reaction.

"Does it make you feel you would like to stay here forever?"

"Sort of, though it might prove lonely eventually."

He laughed, "Yes, perhaps it would."

Later in the afternoon, they sat in front of the cabin enjoying the heat of the sun. He asked if she brought a swimsuit. She did. That prompted a change of clothing soon followed by a dive into the reasonably warm lake. The swim invigorated them and made drying off in the sun even more enjoyable.

For dinner, John brought out wood from behind the cabin to build a fire in an old brick barbecue. Once the initial flames died down, he placed two baked potatoes wrapped in foil on top.

"At the risk of alienating you with my doctor's hat on, did you know that aluminum can leach out of that foil?"

"No. Is that bad?"

"Studies have shown that aluminum collects in the brain and destroys brain cells which can lead to senility or worse."

"Does that mean you won't eat one of those?"

"No," she laughed, "it takes a lot of them to be a problem. An easy way to erase any concern is to wrap the potato in parchment paper inside the foil."

"I'll do that next time."

"It becomes more of a problem when people wrap marinated meat or fish in foil before cooking. The acid increases the chance of leaching aluminum out."

"These steaks come seasoned but unwrapped." They began to sizzle on the barbecue. The aroma increased both appetites.

After dinner, they sat outside and watched the sun set. A loon's haunting cry echoed across the lake. Cynthia was at peace with the world.

"Perhaps I could stay here forever," she said. He laughed.

# Chapter 18

Sylvia called Cynthia. No answer. *She must have gone out this evening or perhaps they called her in to work.* They were both busy now and schedule clashes were inevitable. She would call again in the morning if she didn't hear from Cynthia.

She recalled with pleasure the warm greeting they received on their return to Tahsis with Tommy. Even Delbert, familiar with her ability to win friends, was impressed. He spent two hours with James Wakium describing how to build both a cold box to germinate seeds and a greenhouse. He left plans for the greenhouse with James and promised to supply a roll of transparent film. James showed them the proposed garden area. It looked ideal. Sylvia felt optimistic about the project.

And yesterday, news had traveled fast from one village to another. They called her Sister Sylvia and treated her with a respect that bordered on reverence, which bothered her.

On the good side, it made her introduction simple and effective. So many people descended on her they had to stay overnight to make sure all children were up to date with inoculations. Early cases were genuine, but she sensed a transition to curiosity seekers who simply wanted to meet her. She gently scolded those in good health in a friendly way. She didn't want to alienate anyone. Delbert teased her about her new-found fame on the west coast.

* * *

"Sorry, there's no lighting in the cabin other than candles. I usually turn in when it gets dark."

"That's fine with me. The fresh air and exercise has left me ready for a solid sleep. Thanks for introducing me to your hidden Eden."

She half expected him to suggest they sleep together and found herself attracted by the idea. But he made no move in that direction. She reconciled herself to sleeping alone on one of the two cots. *Is he just shy or determined to go slow? He doesn't exhibit the attraction I usually generate in men. Am I losing my allure?* Not likely, she thought with amusement.

Her thoughts of sex rapidly disappeared as she fell into a sound sleep. An hour later, she dreamed there was an engine starting. Suddenly, her senses were jarred awake. It was an engine. She heard the unmistakeable sound of an airplane starting to taxi away and leaped from the bed toward the door only to fall headfirst on the floor. *What the hell?* She reached down to the leg that stopped her and felt a chain attached to it.

"John," she shouted, "what's going on?"

No answer other that the airplane roar during takeoff. She reached out to the other cot. Empty. She pulled on the chain. It was fastened to the wall under her bed. Her mind churned. *What's he up to? Will he come back in the morning? Why chain me? Is he afraid I might wander off while he's gone and get lost? Why didn't he just tell me he had to go back?* A more sinister thought crept in. *Is he abandoning me? Trying to teach me what it feels like? I already know what it feels like.* It made no sense.

She sat on the cot and tried to think things out. Panic was not the answer. Stay calm as best she could. It wasn't the first predicament she encountered and wouldn't be the last. Her optimistic nature said it would work out. Yet, it was a serious predicament, no escaping that.

An almost full moon lit up the lake and clearing. For two hours, she sat and listened for an approaching plane that did not come. Exhaustion finally forced her into a fitful sleep. Wide awake at dawn, she searched what sky she could see from her reach within the cabin. No sign of John. Surely, he would return and rescue her from this nightmare.

Thirsty, she looked for water or pop. Nothing within reach. She inspected the chain. It was sturdy and the eye bolt fastened to the wall did not yield when she pulled the chain. The clamp on her leg obviously had no release.

The extent of her danger grew more apparent. Left with no food or water, she must rely on his mercy. Not a comfortable prospect. Her thoughts turned again to the question of why.

*Perhaps I could stay here forever.* The thought hit her with a vengeance. *That's what I said. Does it make you feel you would like to stay here forever?* He had asked the question. Was that his intention all along? *Why?* She began to recall the times when his body language had left her slightly uneasy.

*Is he leaving me to starve to death, to disappear without a trace like his mother? His mother—his mother who had resorted to prostitution to raise them—prostitution! I told him I was a drug addicted prostitute for half a year. Did the men every night drive him to a hatred for what his mother did? My God! Did he kill his own mother here?* The full import staggered her.

It took long minutes and deep breaths to regain control. Now she knew her only hope for survival lay in escape. The chance of anyone coming to the cabin or even searching for her in this area was a pipe dream. Probably no one had seen them leave together. It was apparent now why John moored his plane at a little private float up the river just past the ballpark. If only she had reached her parents and told them she was flying here for the weekend. John didn't know they now lived in Campbell River. He simply gambled that she had told nobody they were coming here this weekend and won.

She shuddered at the thought of his mother buried somewhere outside. What a horrible slow death he had in mind. It would take two to three weeks to die, with days of agony. How could she escape?

The chain proved unbreakable. Her knowledge of anatomy didn't offer any way of surgically cutting her foot to allow it to slide through the band. Besides, there was no knife and even if she succeeded, she couldn't walk away. The bolt was the only alternative. But it was firmly attached to the wall. She was unable to turn it. She sat on the bed and cried.

# Chapter 19

Still no answer on Sunday morning. Strange, Sylvia thought. The hospital must have needed her to fill in this weekend. On a whim, she decided to drive by Cynthia's apartment on her way to the grocery store. That created a mystery since Cynthia's car was parked outside. Sylvia stopped and knocked. No answer. Cynthia was conscientious about advising them of her schedule.

She decided to return from the store via the hospital just for reassurance. The receptionist checked the staff log and said Cynthia was not on duty. *Where can she be?* It was time to make Delbert aware of the situation.

"What should we do? She seems to have just disappeared."

"Let's report her missing in case she really is."

"Do you think she may have had a relapse?"

"After all these years, it would be highly unlikely. Besides, we haven't seen any sign of that. She's not under any real stress, enjoys her job."

"True. It's just hard to think of another explanation."

Delbert called the police station. A Mountie said he would come over and interview them to get details.

Later, Jack McCain promised to canvas her neighbourhood for clues and report back. No one had anything to offer. Many only knew her by sight or not at all. A few in her apartment building had talked to her on occasion, John being one of them.

Jack paid more attention to him since he was about Cynthia's age. Also, Jack knew he was Joe's brother, even though that smacked of guilt by association.

"Do you know Doctor Cynthia Adams?"

"In apartment five? Yes, we've met."

"When did you last see her?"

John thought for a moment. "Saturday morning. She headed out for a walk."

"Which way did she go?"

"Afraid I didn't pay a lot of attention. Think she headed up the road."

"You haven't seen her since or heard anyone else mention her?"

"No."

"Thank you. If you see or hear anything, call us."

"Did something happen to her?"

"Not that we know of."

\* \* \*

*Quit crying and feeling sorry for yourself. There must be a way to get free.* Cynthia surveyed the room in detail, checked her range in all directions from the bolt. There was nothing but the two cots. She had to find something to unscrew the bolt. Maybe something on a cot. She pealed back blankets and mattress from John's. It had an old-fashioned set of horizontal springs, not much to work with.

It did have fold-up legs held in place by a flat bar that pivoted on a rivet at one end. It was easy to unlatch the bar but the rivet held it on the frame. She grasped the free end and pulled. The bar bent slightly but held firm. She braced her feet against the frame and tugged with all her might. It simply bent further. Frustrated, she worked it back and forth, wrenched it repeatedly until it showed signs of loosening. A hint of success encouraged her to pull harder again and again. It appeared to be giving up the battle. Finally, it popped off sending her sprawling backward.

She had a tool! Only, there seemed no way to use it on the bolt. No room to pass it through the eye. It looked as though it could be forced through a chain link. *Can I use it to twist the first link and get it to turn the bolt?* She pulled the chain straight out from the bolt and twisted it with her hand. It would transfer the force to the bolt. It proved easy to insert the latch end of the bar and twist it to grip the link. That encouraged her.

With one hand holding the chain link, she pulled on the outer end of the bar. Nothing happened. She pulled harder, then used a series of wrenching tugs that hurt her hand. The bolt rotated a little! She pulled as hard as she could and was rewarded with motion. After extracting the bar and inserting it in the opposite side of the link, the bolt turned more readily. Excited now, she worked quickly. Suddenly, it turned so easily the bar was not needed. But she soon realized the bolt was not coming out.

The fact that it was a bolt and not a lag screw dawned on her. It must go right through the wall and be fastened with a nut on the outside. That meant the nut was now spinning with the bolt. Crestfallen, she sat back to think. The nut had to be pulled tight against the wall to generate needed friction. She braced herself to tug on the chain as she turned it. Nothing happened in the first quarter turn. Then she felt more resistance. It must have caught! She willed herself to work slowly, carefully. It seemed to go on forever. Then the bolt came free sending her falling backward again with a sense of euphoria. She was no longer a prisoner.

*Calm down. You're still over seventy-five miles from civilization.* She dragged the chain around the room in search of things to help. A can of ginger ale slaked her thirst. There was nothing to cut the chain off. She ate an orange and some bread. He had left the provisions brought in, simply chained her and departed. There were two raw eggs for breakfast. She decided they were for show in case she inspected the chest. He didn't plan on cooking a breakfast for two.

A new thought popped into her head. What if he came back to check on her? He would have to kill her immediately. She needed to get away from the cabin. Dressing with the chain was a challenge. She had to feed it through the leg of her shorts before pulling them up. Once dressed and with her sneakers on, she lifted the chain over her shoulder, left the cabin and hiked up the path they had traveled yesterday. It was in the right direction. She repeatedly scanned the sky for an approaching airplane, ready to scuttle into the undergrowth if necessary.

The path ended at the hilltop. Moving down the far side showed it would be no easy hike out. At places, she could walk on moss or grass but that was interspersed with heavy undergrowth. Often the chain caught on things and pulled against her shoulder. Rawness and bruising turned into an agonizing blister. All day she slogged on, stopping only once to rest and drink the other can of ginger ale. It became obvious she would have to find water and something to eat in the days ahead. Her hope of covering twenty miles a day looked too ambitious.

Late in the afternoon, she encountered a lake and decided to work around it to her left. The underbrush was thicker here, probably due to the moisture. Ten minutes later she broke into a clearing. Her jaw dropped, blood drained from her face as she stared at the cabin.

# Chapter 20

Sunday evening and still no word from Cynthia. The Mountie reported back that she had been seen Saturday morning headed out for a walk. After patrolling all the roads, she might have taken, he was organizing a search party. He had the apartment manager let him into her apartment. No sign of anything unusual there. He took a piece of unwashed clothing to give tracking dogs a scent. They would take the dogs along the likely roads in the morning to see if they could find some trace of her.

Sylvia cancelled all her appointments for the next three days. She and Delbert took off in Delboat to fly a search pattern that expanded gradually out from town. They kept on though it seemed more and more like an exercise in futility as the day wore on. A sense of dread grew to the point where a relapse became almost preferable to the alternatives that weighed on them.

\* \* \*

Tears flowed down her cheeks. A whole day wasted traveling in a circle. At least there was no seaplane tied to the float. *What if he came back and found me gone? He would frantically search for me.* She scanned the lake that was visible to her in case he lurked out there. No sign of him. It would be too dangerous to spend a night in the cabin. She worked her way back into the woods, careful not to leave a trail.

It was cold huddled under a cedar tree. Sleep was so fitful it felt like she was awake all night. Once she flinched in terror when an owl hooted nearby. Dawn brought a measure of relief, but the full impact of hiking out scared her. Travel must be in a straight line, warmth at night was needed, water and food were essential. It was daunting but she had no choice.

Return to the cabin was risky yet it had some of what she needed. She had not heard an airplane but knew he could glide to a landing with the engine idling. Or he could swoop in and land before she could get away again. Still, she had to chance it. She moved quietly back to the edge of the clearing. A scan of the sky and water indicated she was alone. After a deep breath, she lifted the chain and ran to the cabin.

Inside, it was as she had left it. He had not come back. She rummaged through cupboards and found two cans containing flour and sugar. Two chocolate bars were hidden behind them. There was also a quart bottle with a screw cap. After making sure she was still alone, she ran to the stream and filled the bottle. Back in the cabin, she emptied non-essentials from her purse, tossed in the bars, then poured in sugar. With the smallest blanket available wrapped around her, she set off up the path again.

At the top of the hill, she used the morning sun to orient her back along the course they had flown. It took a minute to find a landmark to aim for, a tall, scraggly snag on the next hill. She started toward it and checked her course every time she glimpsed it.

In less than thirty minutes, the pain in her shoulder made her stop. She couldn't go on this way. Fear mounted. Once again, she willed herself to quell it, to reason her way to a solution. The answer was to fold the blanket in half lengthwise and wrap it around the chain to form a pad. It dawned on her that she should bring the chain up her back to the opposite shoulder. Not only would it unload the sore side, the chain passing behind her would make it less prone to tripping her.

By mid-morning she stood under her landmark and searched for a new target. A rock outcrop somewhat right of what she wanted would work if she passed a thousand feet or so to its left. This time the valley was denser. She lost sight of the rock and when she finally saw it again, she was too far left. She set a course directly toward it, amazed at how quickly one became disoriented in the woods. Nearer the rock, she turned back on her desired course and climbed to the crest of the hill to search for a new landmark. There wasn't one. The sun directly overhead provided no guidance.

With no sense of direction, it was foolhardy to press on. A shady spot under a tree gave her a cool place to rest until the sun started down again. She ate one of the chocolate bars and drank half the water. She needed to find more water before dark. In the meantime, she dozed off.

Two hours later, the sun position gave confidence in her ability to maintain the desired direction. She set off once more. It proved slow going. On the bright side, she encountered a small lake that allowed her to drink to her heart's content and refill the bottle. She pressed on until sunset, then found a safe place to sleep, curled up in her blanket, out like a light.

* * *

Delbert and Sylvia returned home discouraged and distressed. The search turned up nothing. Jack told them the dogs had not picked up a scent so far. They were expanding the search. Sylvia notified the hospital of Cynthia's plight so they could reschedule to cover her absence. She prayed for Cynthia to be found safe and sound.

Delbert provided police with a photograph and a missing person bulletin went out. Police would look for her up and down the island which was little comfort but better than nothing. He thought the dogs were still their best chance of tracking her down. It was hard to suppress the fear that she was lying hurt somewhere—or worse.

* * *

Cynthia was off again as soon as the sun peeked over the trees. Weary and sore from yesterday, it took an hour to loosen up. The sun's warmth helped. She estimated she had traveled about fifteen miles but realized that might be optimistic. Perhaps she could make better time today. She never stopped scanning the sky and listening for an airplane.

*What if someone else flies by? Will I be able to tell for sure it isn't him? Even if it's not a Cessna, can I be sure it isn't him? No point in worrying about that until one comes.*

She struggled on for three hours, using landmarks as targets when possible and the sun position when not. At one point, she encountered a creek and replenished her water supply. The second chocolate bar was eaten for energy and already she was hungry again. The next few days would be difficult, even torturous. She had to press on but right then rest was more important. She found some shade and slumped down to wait for the sun to pass over.

From mid afternoon until dusk, she labored on, stopping briefly only when needed to check or reset her course. Evening found her climbing a modest mountain. Her energy sapped, it was slow going, further impeded by frequent rest stops. She had to quit for the day before the summit was reached.

Dawn Wednesday morning found her still exhausted. Something caused her hair to bristle. She felt watched. *Is it him?* Trembling, she peered out from under her tree. A cougar stared at her, not forty feet away. *Does it think I am easy prey? How can I scare it?* She raised the chain and flung its end to the ground. Links that hit rocks clanked. With a defiant glare, she lifted it for a second blow. The cougar bolted.

The encounter left her shaken. Would it return or maybe trail her until she was too weak to fight it off? She needed energy. Time to dip into the sugar hoarded in her purse. Dissolved in water, it provided enough sustenance to get her started again. For how long, she couldn't tell. Survival instinct drove her forward, carrying her blanket wrapped chain, bottle and purse. A cliff provided a landmark that let her press on when the sun was too high to give direction. She fell, worn out, in a hollow halfway to the cliff.

An hour's rest revived her slightly. *I need food—and water.* But where? She got to her feet and looked around. Off to her left, she thought she saw a glint of water. It turned out to be a small pond choked with algae. On the far side, a stream trickled in. It was enough to fill the bottle, drink half and fill again.

For the first time, she noticed a wild blackberry patch next to the pond. She attacked it with a vengeance, devouring all that were easily reached. Her medical training reined in the gorging and prompted her to fill the purse for future use. A momentary concern that a bear might happen by and take umbrage at her theft of its food supply made her laugh for the first time in three days. She set off toward the cliff again.

By dusk, she was tired but satisfied with the day's progress. Surely it was close to twenty miles, especially with the speed made on the downside of the mountain during the morning hours. With no sign of the cougar all day, she slept soundly.

# Chapter 21

Another day's search turned up nothing. How could she simply drop off the face of the earth without a trace? It didn't make sense. Someone must have spotted her. If she wandered off a road into the woods, the dogs would have picked up her scent. They found nothing.

Neither Delbert nor Sylvia could believe she had turned back to drugs. She had too much common sense, too strong a character to fall back. The thought that she had been abducted surfaced often. Who would do that? And why? They had to face the possibility that a psychopath had grabbed and murdered her. It was a gruesome thought. They repeatedly shied away from it. But the chance of finding her alive dwindled with each passing day.

They barely slept Wednesday night. Early in the morning, Delbert set off on his fruitless search again. He had to. There was nothing else he could do. For her part, Sylvia drove the car up and down roads in search of some clue, to no avail. With no sign of her, the police began to suspect she had somehow drowned in a lake or the ocean. They concentrated their effort in that direction.

*  *  *

Thursday, Cynthia woke with more energy than she had previous days. A mixture of water, berries and sugar formed a fair breakfast. She set off determined to make even better progress than yesterday. Already athletic, her muscles were now hardening. It would be important to watch for more berries and water. For the first time, she felt optimistic about her chance of survival.

Her spirits were further buoyed by the terrain, which was more open. An hour later, those spirits were dashed. She heard an airplane approaching and dived for cover under a tree. *Is it him? Can he see me here?* She checked to be sure nothing shiny showed, particularly the chain. Now she wished she had taken the green blanket. The plane passed over to the right of her crouched, trembling figure.

After it passed, she peeked out. It was a float plane, perhaps a Cessna, she couldn't tell. The colours looked different than what she remembered. At least, it didn't turn back. *Just the thought of him terrifies me. How can an evil man have such a strong effect? If I get out of this alive, will it scar me for life? I can't let it.*

When it was obvious the floatplane would not return, she started off again. Periodically she scanned the sky behind her. When the sun was overhead, she followed her pattern of resting for a couple of hours. The sun was her compass. She was grateful that the warm weather held. A cloud cover would make navigation difficult if not impossible at times.

Partway through the afternoon, she came across what could be called a big pond or a small lake. The water was clear. Nearby, there were blackberries like before. She ate and drank, then restocked purse and bottle. She made good progress for the rest of the day.

Friday morning, the pattern continued. Her spirits soared in the afternoon when she spotted smoke on the horizon. It could be the pulp mill. Half an hour later, she hit a road. *What should I do? Follow the road or keep on through the woods?* On the road, someone might come along and give her a ride. Would they believe her story or be scared off by the chain, thinking she might be an escaped convict? What if he came along?

On the other hand, the road was inviting. Easy to walk and certain to lead to civilization. She decided to follow the road and leap into the bushes if she heard a car approach. None did. At dusk, she felt more confident on the road. She would see car lights in plenty of time to hide. At each junction, she chose the road that headed east. She began to pass scattered houses and was tempted to knock on a door to seek help. She kept on instead.

It was close to midnight when roads changed to streets. Eventually she got her bearings and steered a wide berth away from her apartment. She wanted to be nowhere near the monster. When a car came by, she ducked off the street behind a hedge. Other than that, the streets were empty. Occasionally a dog barked. She hurried on, desperate to reach her parents. They must have known she was missing by now.

Exhausted, she finally reached their house. She rang the doorbell and crouched out of sight from the street. *Does John know I escaped? If he knows, he will be watching to intercept me. He must kill me at this point. I can't fail now.* She rang the doorbell again, then pounded on the door. *Wake up! Wake up!*

A light came on. Sylvia opened the door thinking it was a prank.

"Mum."

"Thia! Thia!" She hugged the girl. Felt the chain.

"Inside," Cynthia urged.

When the door was closed, Sylvia shouted, "Delbert! It's Thia!". She cried—a mixture of relief and joy.

Cynthia discarded the dirty blanket, bottle and purse. They hugged again. Tears flowed.

"We've been so worried. What happened? Are you alright? You look terrible. Why the chain?"

Cynthia laughed with a release of tension and feeling of safety at long last. "I'll explain."

Delbert rolled in, a wide smile on his face. The chain and her dirt, scratches and torn clothing sobered him. They held hands, firmly.

"Thank God you're safe!"

She nodded and began to relate her story. They were horrified.

"We need to get that chain off," Sylvia insisted.

"No," Delbert countered, "not yet. We need the police to see it and gather whatever evidence is needed to charge this psychopath. I'll report in."

"Guess you're right. If I can't take a bath, can I at least have some tea and maybe a sandwich?"

"Of course. I'll fix it."

# Chapter 22

Delbert gave the Mountie on duty a condensed version of Cynthia's story.

"I'm going to wake Sergeant McCain. Give me your address. He will want to come over to get her story as soon as possible, if that's okay?"

"Yes, of course."

"We're very glad she's alright. To be honest, we feared the worst."

Delbert told the women the Mountie would be over as soon as the night officer could wake him.

"Perhaps we should trade these pajamas for clothes before he arrives. How are you feeling, Thia? Can I get you anything?"

"I'm fine now. Go change."

*  *  *

"Doctor Adams—"

"Cynthia."

"Cynthia, it's a relief to find you alive and well."

"It's a relief for me too," she laughed.

He took out a notepad and asked her to tell the story from beginning to end. She did but avoided the prostitution link, simply stated the opinion that his mother might have suffered the fate intended for her. Like her parents, he shuddered at the thought of a dead mother possibly buried near the cabin. More than once he shook his head as the story unfolded. When finished, he said the prosecutor would want to tape her story later. For now, he asked permission to photograph the chain. He stretched it out and stepped back to get it all in the picture. Then he took close-up photos of each end.

"That shackle won't be easy to remove. If you can tolerate it until morning, I'll have a locksmith look at it."

"That's fine. The chain and I are not exactly friends, but we have learned to tolerate each other."

He smiled. "You're a remarkable woman, Doctor."

"Cynthia."

"Cynthia."

\* \* \*

At dawn, Jack knocked on John Carson's door.

"Yes Sir, have you found that woman?"

"We have."

A look of shock slipped for an instant across John's face.

"You have the right to remain silent. Anything you say may be used against you in a court of law. You have the right to be represented by legal counsel."

"What's this all about?" he blustered.

"You are under arrest on a charge of attempted murder. Turn around. I suggest you remain silent."

Jack pulled each hand back and cuffed him.

\* \* \*

Before the locksmith took a shot at freeing Cynthia, Jack dusted the shackle for fingerprints. He expected any prints would belong to Cynthia but it was worth a try. The locksmith inspected the shackle closely.

"It's a tough one. Don't suppose the culprit will give you a key?"

"You're on your own, Sam."

He took out what appeared to be a pair of small knitting needles and began prodding. An ell shaped needle followed. He worked delicately for fifteen minutes until finally the shackle popped open. He stood up with a look of triumph. Cynthia was too busy rubbing her chafed shin to notice.

"I hesitate to ask this, Cynthia. Do you think you could lead us back to the cabin?"

"Yes."

"Good. Then I will arrange for a seaplane to take us."

Delbert spoke up. "I'll take you," he said with authority.

Jack looked at him quizzically.

"I have a flying boat moored at the seaplane dock. We can go in that."

"Yes, I want Dad there."

"Fine."

"Can I take a bath now?" They all nodded with a laugh.

* * *

Jack showed up at the ramp with a large dog.

"Hope we can take King along? He's a talented blood hound."

"With King here, can Sergeant Preston be far behind?"

"Very funny. Guess we deserve that."

Delbert turned serious. "We can put King behind me on a leash as long as he doesn't attack me inflight."

He rolled onboard and turned back to face the dog when it was urged to enter. He petted the dog and scratched it behind the ears. They decided to be friends. Delbert turned to the controls as Cynthia raised the ramp. He soon had the plane facing the other direction so they could board. King was obviously glad to have Jack close by again.

"You fly it, Thia. You know where we're headed. It's been a while since you've logged any hours."

"You're a pilot too?"

"Dad taught me to fly before I flew off to university."

Jack became uneasy in the back seat as they taxied out. The lack of engine noise was disturbing rather than a comfort. He knew this weird vehicle had flown before but wondered if it would again despite assurances from the pair up front. Cynthia on the controls didn't help his confidence. That all melted away once airborne and he could begin to appreciate the quiet ride. Even King seemed to enjoy his new view as he sat up and stared out the side window.

Cynthia turned to the heading she saw before. In about forty minutes, they should be in the lake's vicinity. Delbert tracked their progress on a map and named the lakes they passed. Some sounded familiar but none looked like the one they sought. When they must have passed it, Delbert asked what wind they had that day.

"There was almost no wind."

"We've been pushed north today. Let's fly back five miles south of here."

They were only on the reverse course five minutes when Delbert said, "There's a lake with a cabin on the east side."

"Good old eagle eyes. The one at two o'clock?"

"Yes."

They descended toward the small lake he pointed out. She agreed it was their goal when she got a good view of the cabin. She circled to land. Jack was again uneasy, secretly wished Delbert would take over. King became restless when they splashed down and threw up spray near his window. Calm returned as the plane slowed to taxi in. Soon all were on land. Jack took photographs of the cabin and clearing. Cynthia stopped in front of the cabin. She shook, clearly afraid to enter. Jack put his hand on her arm.

"He's locked in a cell in Campbell River."

"I'm sorry. It's an involuntary reaction. I know better. Give me a moment to calm down." The dog licked her other hand which broke the tension in her body.

"Thanks, King. You're a smart fellow." She put her hand on his neck and they moved forward.

Inside, nothing had changed. He had never come back. That thought caused Cynthia to shudder. Jack asked them to wait while he photographed everything. He paid special attention to the cot, bent bar and bolt hole, then the provisions and open sugar canister. Satisfied, he went outside to locate the bolt hole and photographed it and the fallen nut. Finally, he shot the stream and path up the hill.

"That covers it. Now for the gruesome part."

He led King behind the cabin and signalled he wanted the ground sniffed. The dog understood. They traced a pattern back and forth around the cabin in an ever-increasing radius. Nothing detected. They started up the path, working from side to side. Suddenly King stopped, barked quietly, and scratched the grass. They returned to the front of the cabin where the other two sat.

"Please stay here or in the plane."

He retrieved a shovel from the cabin and headed back up. Thirty minutes later he returned.

"Two bodies are buried up there."

Cynthia gasped. *I could be there.* Delbert held her hand for comfort. Jack went back up with two evidence bags and his camera. He was gone another ten minutes.

"We can leave. I reburied them for now," he said. They were not about to ask what the bags contained. Even left to their imagination, they were sickened.

The flight home was uneventful and the beauty outside revived their spirits somewhat. Before they parted company in Campbell River, Jack took a moment to reassure Cynthia.

"Between our collected evidence and his menace, there is no chance Carson will be let out on bail but if for some unforeseen reason bail is granted, I will let you know."

King gave Cynthia one last lick before parting.

# Chapter 23

Monday morning Cynthia reported in at the hospital. The receptionist greeted her with a look of curiosity.

"We missed you last week?"

"Yes, I had a problem and was unable to call in. Do you have my schedule for this week?"

"They took you off the schedule since no one knew where you were."

A familiar voice called from the entrance, "Cynthia! Where have you been? We were informed you had gone missing."

"It's a long, sad story."

"I've got some time," Doctor Munson offered. "Come into my office."

She followed him. "Don't know how much the police want me to disclose. Can we consider the details confidential?"

"Sure—unless you're running from some horrible crime."

His smile relaxed her. "Oddly enough, that's exactly what I was doing, only I was the intended victim."

That piqued his curiosity. "Tell me what you can."

She related her experience in general terms with all names omitted. The shock showed on his face.

"That's astounding. I take it the abductor is in jail?"

"For the time being at least."

"I should think for a long time. You were alone in the backwoods six days without gear, hiking out?"

"Yes. Well, the first day was wasted because I walked in a circle right back to the cabin. I can almost laugh at that now."

"Remarkable. It must have been terrifying. Why did he single you out?"

"It was terrifying." She hesitated to weigh how much to tell him. He always supported her. Would he continue if he found out she had been a prostitute? Could he understand how drug addiction destroyed valuable lives? For that matter, would he still trust her as a doctor if he knew she was once addicted? She hated to keep it secret. That made her feel like it was all her fault. Being open with people had always proved beneficial, except with John.

"Doctor Munson, I greatly admire how you operate. You have become a role model for me. However, what I'm about to tell you may test you severely. I certainly hope not."

"If you tire of medicine, you could make a fortune as a mystery writer with your knack of creating suspense," he laughed.

"I will never tire of medicine. At the end of Grade eleven, my parents abandoned me, sent me to live with my father's brother on Salt Spring Island. He was an evil man. Without my understanding the peril, he managed to get me addicted to heroin."

Munson's eyed her with surprise.

"For half a year, I supported the habit as a prostitute in Victoria. Delbert Pillage found me in a gutter. He and Sylvia rescued me using methadone which I took for three years before I could move on without it. They put me through medical school. I consider them my parents and am thankful to them every day."

"Are you free of the addiction now?"

"I have not touched a drug in eight years. Sometimes I worry that I have an addictive personality trait. I never smoke or drink alcohol just to be careful."

"You really are a survivor. Do you find yourself addicted to other things? Chocolates? Some form of exercise, perhaps?"

She laughed, "No. I won't turn down a chocolate, but I don't crave them."

"What about work? Medical school almost requires an addiction to study?"

"It takes drive and perseverance but not addiction."

"True. Frankly, I think your personality leans in that direction rather than addiction. Doesn't mean you should try cigarettes and alcohol. Be thankful you have avoided them. What I don't understand is why you are telling me all this?"

"Prostitution was the link. He hated prostitution. His mother had used it to support him and his brother through their teen years. I made the mistake of being candid with him."

"I see...thank you for trusting me. Rest assured I have no intention of doing away with you." He grinned slightly. "In fact, until now I have simply been impressed with your work. Now, I admire you greatly as a person. You are a truly remarkable young woman—and a fine doctor."

"Thank you." Her eyes glistened slightly.

"I'll see that you are put back on the schedule."

\* \* \*

The hospital superintendent asked why she missed all last week.

"It was a very serious personal issue."

"That's all you are going to tell me?"

"That's all. In time, it will become common knowledge and you will probably enjoy television crews running around here for interviews."

"Damn it Doc, you whet my curiosity and clam up?"

"Sorry."

* * *

On Thursday Jack called Cynthia. He knew she had moved in with her parents after returning to the apartment only long enough to pack her things.

"Carson has been transferred to the jail in Nanaimo. He will be tried down there. A forensic team has gathered all they need in the way of evidence. The prosecutor told me your story is well borne out by it."

Cynthia asked hesitantly, "Were the bodies identified?"

"Yes. One was a young woman that went missing a year and a half ago. The other was his mother."

Cynthia paused to steady herself and rein in her emotion. "Thank you."

# Chapter 24

"It's been hot and dry for over a month now."

"A statement like that always means something's on your mind, dear."

Delbert laughed. "Yes, forest fires to be exact."

"Are you planning to turn Delboat into a water bomber?"

"That's surprisingly close to what I have in mind."

"Delbert, you've bucked enormous odds many times but you can't take on a forest fire."

"Course not but I saw two giant flying boats that can sitting on Sproat Lake just west of Port Alberni. They're fairly new Martin Mars amphibians."

"Do you think they will let you fly one?"

"No, no. I couldn't reach the rudder pedals. What I have in mind is scouting for fires. When I spot one, I can guide them to it and nip it in the bud."

"They have rangers out spotting fires."

"At points, yes. The coverage is thin. Fires often have a head start on the bombers."

"Sounds like they could use you."

"It'll be something useful to do while waiting for you."

Tacit approval or at least acceptance from Sylvia was all he needed to set off in Delboat for Port Alberni. He landed on

Sproat Lake and taxied to the dock in front of two giant brothers parked on the ramp. A man on the float walked over.

"This isn't a public dock, buddy."

"I want to talk to someone in charge about doing some fire spotting for you people."

Delbert threw mooring lines out the window. The man tied them off. "Talk to the boss inside."

His jaw dropped along with Delbert's ramp when he saw the wheelchair. "You're Delbert Pillage?"

"That's right."

"George McBride. I was an aero mechanic stationed in Comox when you were there. Attended your award ceremony. It was the most moving experience of my life when you flew that missing comrade pass."

"That was quite a few years ago."

"Yesterday to me. Had tears in my eyes when you hugged Chuck Lansbury after he caused your crash. Chuck's a good friend."

"Haven't seen him in months."

"He comes by occasionally. I tell him he should fly the Hawaii Mars over there. Terrain following in that big Mama takes real skill. Follow me."

They both laughed. The one step into the building halted them. Delbert spun around to back up to it.

"Can I pull you up?"

"I can manage." He rocked one wheel up, leaned the other way to pull the second one up. George shook his head. "You're a real pro with that thing."

"Over eight years of practice—I should have learned a few tricks."

Inside, he introduced Delbert to Frank Hollaman and couldn't resist talking about his role as the jet pilot who created the Pillager squadrons.

"I've heard about you. Great to meet you. Pardon me for being a smart ass but are you looking for a job flying one of the Mars boys?"

Delbert laughed. "I enjoyed flying some similar patrol aircraft years ago but, as I told my wife, I might have a hell of a time reaching the rudder pedals now."

Frank sobered. "Yeah. Damn shame."

"There is something I could do for you. I often have time on my hands. I could spend it searching for fires. Maybe get them located earlier so you can attack them while they're still small."

"Interesting. How would you do that?"

"My little flying boat outside looks like a mosquito next to the water bombers but it can fly all day without refueling."

Frank looked at the strange little machine.

"I'm not about to turn down an offer that might save acres of timber. Don't know how much we can pay you until we give it a try."

"I don't want any money. If it improves your service, that's reward enough."

"Let's give it a shot. Welcome aboard, Delbert. George can fill you in on communication frequencies and protocol. I'll tell the pilots so they won't be surprised if—when they hear from you."

They shook hands. George gave him a tour around the two Martin Mars aircraft, explained how they work and gave him the communication information. Delbert wanted desperately to see the flight deck but getting him up onboard would be too much of an imposition.

George told him with pride, "They pick up six thousand gallons while skimming the lake and when they drop all that water it's a real spectacle."

"Hope I get to see it."

Armed with everything needed, Delbert set off for home. George watched the quiet little flying boat take off, shaking his head sadly once again.

# Chapter 25

The next morning, Delbert and Sylvia set off for Kyuquot on the west coast of the island. This village was even more isolated than Tahsis. Sylvia expected they might meet with a cool welcome after the initial experience at Tahsis. The local people did appear wary of the strangers arriving in a machine different from any before.

Sylvia's disarming smile prompted them to guide her to the village leader where she described once again her reason for the visit as a public health nurse. The chief claimed most were in good health.

"Most?"

"One family has been cursed with a fatal illness. Already the eldest son is dead. Others will follow."

"Where are they? I must find out why."

"Why is in the hands of the spirits. You should not go there."

"I must. That's my job."

He shook his head.

"Point out their house," she insisted.

He sensed the stubbornness in her voice and decided he had warned her sufficiently.

"If you won't heed my advice, follow me."

He led her up a barely gravelled road roughly two thousand yards and pointed to a small shack. Sylvia knocked on the door. A wild looking man opened it and stared at the young woman dressed all in white with her black kit bag on one arm.

"Who are you?"

"Sylvia Pillage, a nurse. I want to check your family."

"Go away."

"I'll stand here until you let me in."

He stared at her, looked past her to the chief standing down the road, then back at her. Finally, he retreated to let her enter. The shack had two rooms. A frail, emaciated woman cowered by the inside door. Her face was covered with red rashes. *Measles!* Sylvia turned back to the outside door and called.

"Chief! They have measles. Send word to my husband on the airplane that I will stay here for one week. He should come back for me then. Tell him there's a measles outbreak. Can I count on you?"

"I will tell him."

"Then come back and call me. No one is to come in this house. That includes you."

He nodded and started off down the hill. Sylvia turned back to the woman.

"You have a disease called measles which you can survive. It is not the work of the spirits. It moves from one person to another by touching each other or the saliva from someone with measles. I need to check your children."

The woman looked toward the inner door. Sylvia passed through and found three children lying in bunk beds. Each was covered with rashes and appeared highly feverish. The oldest boy moaned occasionally. He had suffered from diarrhea which had not been cleaned up. The stench was staggering.

"Put a blanket over that window," she told the father who had followed her. "They need to be kept in darkness to help prevent blindness. Your wife too."

She looked at the woman. "Please lie in your bed. You need rest. I will look after the children."

Both parents followed her instructions, intimidated by this strange woman who dared to defy the spirits in their infested house. Back in the main room she found a chipped porcelain sink with a single faucet. It provided a weak stream of cold water. She filled a small bucket and carried it, along with her kit, into the bedroom. With a compress from her supplies, she began to dab faces with cold water. Clean-up could wait until she had the fevers under control.

Ten minutes later a voice outside called, "Mrs. Sylvia."

She went to the door.

"Your man says he will come back each day to make sure you are alright and asks if he should bring you anything."

"Tell him rubbing alcohol. Also, I need you to have people cook good food for this family and leave it outside the door each day. I will come out and get it. Before putting out the empty dishes, I will wash them. To be safe, they should be washed again in hot water. Anyone who touches the dishes should wash their hands thoroughly afterwards."

"I will make that happen. Your man is worried about your safety."

"Tell him I am fine. Thank you for your help."

She had to wait for her eyes to adjust to the now dark rooms before she could mop brows again.

"I can help with that," the man offered.

"Did you have this disease before, perhaps as a child?"

"No."

"Then you should stay away from them. Go and wash your hands. Don't touch anything your wife or children touched and stay in the other room."

He retreated. Sylvia decided the mother was further along in the disease's progression than the children. At least, she had little fever. The oldest boy suffered the most. Survival would be touch and go. She called to the father, "Can you boil some water?"

"Yes, but I need to start a fire first."

"Fine. I will need some sugar too."

It took half an hour to get boiling water and another fifteen minutes to cool it enough to use. Sylvia pulled an emergency intravenous bag from her kit, dissolved sugar in the water, added vitamin A pills and filled the bag. Soon she had the solution dripping into the boy's arm. She prayed silently that it would allow him to regain consciousness.

A call from outside indicated food had arrived. She noticed a crowd watching from a distance when she retrieved it. Two dogs stood nearby, eyes trained on the food. A man called them off. Inside she put together portions for everyone. The father said to give it all to the others. She insisted it was just as important for him to eat. The younger children had to be coaxed to sit up and eat. The mother resisted to start with but hunger made her give in. Sylvia watched the boy for signs of waking. None appeared.

After the meal, she had the man boil more water to wash the dishes. She placed them outside to dry and be recovered. An hour later the intravenous bag was almost empty. She refilled it. Still no sign of improvement in the boy. The two girls' eyes followed the strange woman in white as she mopped their foreheads and necks. That meant they were not blind, not yet anyway.

"How do you feel?"

"Sore—and hot," one replied.

"You will feel better when we get your fever down. I want you to eat and rest for the next few days. You're all going to get well again."

"Even Joey?"

Sylvia glanced at the boy. "It will be harder for Joey. I hope he will too."

The mother watched the interchange. When Sylvia turned to her, the woman thanked her for helping them. Sylvia said it was her job and went to talk to the man.

"They may have diarrhea after eating. How can they go to the bathroom?"

He gave her a sorrowful look. "We have no bathroom. We use an outhouse in the back."

"They can't go outside during daylight."

He brought out an old, battered bucket. "That will work," she said and took it to the bedroom. She dreaded the next chore. The diarrhea Joey lay in had dried. She lifted his head and pulled the top end of the sheet out, then worked down along his body. In places, it was stuck to him and the mattress. She pried it loose, almost gagging. Once free, she carried it outside.

A boy watched her from down the road. She called to him.

"Have someone bring us clean sheets." He ran off.

The sheets showed up with the evening meal. Before eating, Sylvia wrestled with the boy's clothing. Once naked, she gave him a sponge bath, dried him off on a towel, then worked a clean sheet under him and draped another on top. The moaning had stopped. He showed signs of life though still not awake. She explained to the mother and girls that they were to use the bucket if they needed to go to the bathroom.

With a fire maintained in the stove, Sylvia decided to warm their dinner. The food had a noticeable effect on their spirits. What was once despair turned to hope. She wanted desperately for the boy to wake up and eat. Her improvised intravenous seemed to help. He was breathing regularly now. She washed the dinner dishes and deposited them out front.

"I want to burn that sheet and Joey's clothes," she told the father.

"We can pour some lantern coal oil on them."

"I'll need matches too."

The fire and smoke brought a few villagers to investigate. Sylvia explained that contaminated things must be burned.

Later, she felt the call of nature and decided to take the now partly filled bucket out back. It took fortitude to sit in the outhouse and later empty the bucket. *Is this what I signed up for? Well, they need my help.*

Sleeping arrangement was also a problem. The man should stay out front. She told him to use the old sofa. When he asked where she would sleep, she replied in the bedroom with the sick ones. In the end, she curled up in two clean sheets on the floor, exhausted enough to fall asleep. The hard floor took its toll. She woke up aching the next morning.

# Chapter 26

Delbert fretted all evening. He hated to leave Sylvia alone with strangers—diseased strangers. Cynthia shared his concern; however, she better appreciated the motivation that drove Sylvia.

"What bothers me is that I can't get up that road and check on her."

"I'll go with you tomorrow. You'll have to get me back in time for my afternoon shift."

"Thanks. I can do that."

\* \* \*

Sylvia retrieved their breakfast. As she parcelled out each's portions, one of the girls called. "Joey's awake."

She rushed in to find him staring at them, a curious look on his face. She felt his forehead. Still a fever.

"Good morning, Joey. We need to cool you down and give you some breakfast. Do you think you can eat it?"

He studied her, then shook his head. "I don't know. I hurt."

"You've been very sick but now we want you to get well again. You need food for that."

He looked at the needle in his arm with its connected tube.

"I can take that out now."

She went out front to carry in their breakfast. Appetites were returning. That was a good sign. It took Joey a long time to gather courage to nibble on some toast. Gradually he moved on to a more substantial meal with coaxing from Sylvia and then his mother.

Mid morning there was a knock on the door. Sylvia yelled "Go away."

"Mum, it's me."

"Thia, what are you doing here?"

"Dad brought me to check on you."

"Have you had a measles inoculation?"

"Yes, let me in."

Sylvia opened the door and warned her it was not four-star accommodations. She gave Thia a quick summary of each's health.

"Do you mind if I give them a quick check?"

"You're the doctor."

"I don't know. Looks like you've got everything under control."

They moved from one to another, measured temperatures and inspected rashes. For Joey's turn, Sylvia described his time in a coma and the trouble with diarrhea.

"I've got some pills which will reduce that problem. The others may need them too."

Back in the front room, Cynthia quizzed Sylvia.

"How long do you plan to stay here?"

"Until the rashes heal and they can return to the land of the living without scaring off all the villagers."

"Do you have what you need?"

"The village is very good about dropping off meals—and sheets when I needed them."

"Are you getting enough sleep? You look tired."

"Like I said, it's not four-star. We'll get by."

"Dad is mad that he can't get up here. He's worried about you."

"Tell him everything is fine."

"I'm proud of you." They hugged and Cynthia headed off down the hill.

* * *

The household fell into a regular routine over the next three days. Sylvia was delighted when the father began emptying the bucket for her. He still showed no symptoms of the disease, and they were now beyond the contagious period. All were eating well and the rashes were disappearing. One more day would do it. To be sure, they took down the blankets to let light in again. When the squinting subsided, she asked each if they could see as well as ever. There was no blindness. They were lucky.

She checked them again the next morning. Everyone's skin was clear. She had them all wash carefully and put on clean clothes. The parents were instructed to thoroughly clean the house. She helped them.

"Now I think we should all go down and show everyone you are better and thank them for their help."

They appeared reluctant. She stressed that it was important so they would be accepted back into village life. Hesitantly, they followed her. Word spread through the village like wildfire. A crowd gathered near the dock. They stared, amazed to see the whole family healthy again. Joey received the most scrutiny. They thought he had died. Had this strange woman raised him from the dead?

"Don't be afraid, people. This family is completely cured, thanks to your help. Your food was very important in saving their lives. It's safe to be with them, to touch them, play with them, whatever you want."

People moved forward. There were hugs, handshakes, back pats and laughter. The two parents thanked everyone with tears in their eyes. Finally, they turned to Sylvia and knelt in front of her. She pulled them to their feet and hugged them. The crowd cheered.

"One thing I must ask. Has anyone else developed rashes on their skin?"

The chief responded, "No, we have inspected each other carefully for days now."

"Wonderful."

"On behalf of our village, we thank you, Mrs. Sylvia. You will always be an honoured guest here for the miracle you have worked."

"Thank you, it's my job. We have some time before my husband comes to look at any other concerns people have."

She spent the next hour tending to minor problems. When Delbert picked her up, he was not surprised by the rousing farewell they received.

# Chapter 27

All three enjoyed the warm late summer evening on the deck, gazing out over the ocean. A slight breeze wafted in from the sea to provide a refreshing respite. Occasional seagull squawks reached them from down on the beach. Fishing boats and pleasure craft criss-crossed in front. Further out, a freighter moved silently by from behind Quadra Island.

Cynthia broke their reverie. "There's something I would value your opinion on."

"What's that?"

"I'm not sure where to start…it's a difficult subject."

Both parents, suddenly attentive, waited quietly for her to continue.

"It has to do with the dark side of my life or I should say…" she searched for the right words, "…my relations with men. My experiences during addiction left a scar. I have trouble trusting men and frankly, wonder if I can build a loving relationship with one. In college, dates created friendships but not relationships. I was always guarded. Nothing lasting came of them although I felt the situation gradually improve. John destroyed that and brought out all the old fears."

After a moment of silence, Delbert glanced at Sylvia and said, "We can understand why you feel that way."

"Yes," Sylvia interrupted, "I know exactly how you feel."

Delbert continued, "There are a lot of hurtful, evil people in the world—perhaps most of them men. But there's even more good ones, worthy of trust—and love." Sylvia nodded.

"I'm sorry, Mum. You went through something similar. I shouldn't have brought it up."

"No, you're right to bring it out in the open and face it head on."

"That's your style," Delbert added. "You started this discussion with a request for our opinions. For what it's worth, mine is exactly what Sylvia just said. Face the feeling head on and face men head on as well. Yes, exposing your past to John resulted in calamity and maybe your trials will scare others away too. But you are a beautiful, wonderful woman and there will be men who recognize what you are today, who will prize that regardless of anything in the past. Those, you can trust, safely let love flourish."

"I love the way you get right to the point. That's my recommendation too, Thia. Good men will accept the reality of life's misfortunes and move forward. They are the ones to search out and test."

"You two always pump me up. Maybe I will start with Jack McCain. He asked me to join him for dinner Thursday evening."

"He's a solid citizen."

"And easy on the eyes," Sylvia added. That brought a mock glare from Delbert, a laugh from Cynthia.

*  *  *

"Joe, your brother's in jail."

"What did the righteous little bastard do?"

"Word around town is he kidnapped a woman and left her to die in a cabin up on a lake."

Joe straightened up. "Our old cabin." It was a statement, not a question.

"Didn't know you have a cabin."

"I don't. My old man had one. Used to take us up there when we were kids. Maybe John still flies in."

"You going to help him?"

"If he's got a problem, he can live with it."

"But he's your brother."

"Look Ned, stop calling him my brother. I want nothing to do with him. Don't want people to even know we're related. Got that?"

"Okay. Seems a little cold though."

"Forget it. The last thing we need is public attention."

"You've got a point." He paused. "There's something else being mentioned."

"What?"

"There's a rumour he may have killed his mother."

Joe stared at him, silent for minutes.

"Let them talk. As far as we are concerned, the only thing in common is our last name. Understand?"

"Yeah, okay."

\* \* \*

Jack rang the doorbell at five-thirty on Thursday. Cynthia beat Sylvia to the door.

"Love your outfit. You look fantastic without your chain and blackberry scratches."

"Thank you. I only wear the chain for special occasions."

He laughed as he escorted her to the late model Ford Fairlane. *Glad you think I look fantastic. You do too. Wish I had the nerve to tell you that.*

"Where are we headed?"

"Painter's Lodge."

"You go first class."

"Just trying to impress you. Don't expect it often on my salary," he chuckled.

"I make a little money too. We should go Dutch treat."

"Not tonight."

"So, you do get time off. I began to think you must be on call twenty-four hours a day when they dragged you out of bed that night."

"Yours was a special case that I took the lead on. They had orders to bring me in if anything broke."

"I'm glad—even though you lost sleep."

"It's seldom a nine to five job."

The light banter continued until they arrived at the lodge. The ease with which they conversed surprised Cynthia. Jack seemed so natural, so calm, so confident. He made her feel the same. She often dished out a quick repartee with dates but never with the relaxed feeling now enjoyed.

Seated, the waiter asked if they would like to start with a drink.

"Just tonic on ice with a lime, please."

"I'll have a draft beer," Jack added.

After the waiter left, "You stay clear of alcohol?"

"Yes."

"I hope you don't mind me having a beer?"

"Of course not." She paused. *Is it time for Mum's test? God, I don't want to scare him off on our first date. If I put it off and we develop a rapport, then he fails the test, it would hurt a lot more. I don't know.*

"You seem deep in thought."

*Does it show or are you a mind-reader?* She took a deep breath. "Yes, I was. Jack, I'll be honest. I'm very attracted to you and I'm very afraid you will want to walk out when you hear what I need to tell you."

"You're married?"

She laughed weakly, "No."

"A boyfriend?"

"No, not yet."

"You know how to pique one's curiosity."

"Here goes. When I finished Grade eleven, my parents abandoned me. They sent me to live with an uncle on Salt Spring Island. He was an evil man who took advantage of my vulnerability to get me addicted to heroin."

"People like that are the scum of the earth."

"That's not the worst part. When I realized what happened, I ran away but ended up on the street in Victoria prostituting to buy drugs for half a year." Jack's face reddened. *Is it embarrassment or anger?* "That was the link with John's mother. She used prostitution to raise the two boys. He resented strange men showing up each night."

"The young woman buried with her was known to have engaged in prostitution," he added sadly.

*Am I losing him?* She hurried on, "Anyway, Delbert found me in a gutter. He and Sylvia rescued me, got me on methadone and eventually put me through medical school." *There, he knows it all.* She waited for his reaction.

"They saved your life. I could tell they are great people. Now I know how truly great."

*He only looked at the positive side! Didn't mentioned the bad stuff! I'm falling in love with you, Jack McCain!* She forced herself to calm down.

"It took three years to work off the methadone. I was afraid I have an addictive personality, so I never smoke nor drink. Now I realize I don't have that problem, but I've become accustomed to things this way," she said pointing to the tonic which just arrived.

Jack gazed at her for a couple of minutes. "You are an amazing woman, Cynthia—amazing. You're the strongest woman I have ever encountered. A true survivor in every sense of the word."

"Does that mean we are still friends?"

"I hope more than that. I'm very attracted to you. And I have a little confession to make as well. I was afraid the horror you just went through with Carson might leave scars such as fear he might return or worse that all men are unsafe or at least, might be unsafe. I was afraid you might withdraw from male companionship. I wanted to show you we're not all like that."

"You mean you are being a good Samaritan?"

"Oh, I have a very selfish motivation also."

She laughed. "To be serious for a moment, I did have scars and John re-opened the wound. But it will heal again, thanks to my parents and people like you."

"Good."

They paused to order food from a waiter watching for a break in the conversation to descend on them.

When alone again, Sylvia opened a new conversation, "Let's trade my sordid past for a glimpse at yours."

"I grew up on a farm in Fort St John. A poor one—we grew wheat in the summer and froze to death in the winter. I have two brothers and a sister. When we were old enough to run the farm, Dad took a job on the Peace River Dam construction project. We were better off then. I did well in school but there was no way to pay for college.

"You made fun of King the other day, but it struck close to the truth. I never missed an episode of Sergeant Preston and wanted to become a Mountie. That turned out to be possible."

"I get the feeling you're still happy with the choice?"

"Absolutely."

"Working a farm in Fort St John from an early age doesn't sound like a fun-filled childhood."

"We found time to play. Hockey in the winter, baseball in the summer."

"Bet you were a good athlete."

"Pretty fair pitcher—or maybe there weren't many good hitters. We only had one and a half pitchers. I often pitched double-headers."

She laughed, "Iron-arm Jack."

His attention was drawn to the entrance. She followed his look. Mabel had just walked in on the arm of a man in a flashy sportscoat with slicked down hair. She paused momentarily when she spotted Jack, then approached when she realized the encounter was unavoidable.

"Cynthia, I didn't know you're back in town."

"Hi Mabel. Yes, I'm back."

"You must be Sergeant McCain, the new Mountie."

"You know who I am, Mabel." He stood up.

"This is my friend, Steven Cashman. Steven's a lawyer, also new in town."

They shook hands. The new arrivals moved on to their table after a little small talk. Cynthia leaned forward to prevent being overheard.

"You dated Hot Pants." It was a good-natured accusation.

"Who?"

"Hot Pants Harrigan. That's what we called Mabel in high school."

"Once."

"Did you make it home before morning?"

"Yes, though you make me think I was too much of a gentleman."

"Well, it wasn't because she was too much of a lady."

"That's a little catty, don't you think?"

"You're right. I'm sorry. Let's get back to us."

He was happy to move on. *One good thing, Mabel found a way for me to forget any responsibility for her.* "I was told Delbert ended up in the wheelchair because of an airplane crash?"

"He was a test pilot for the RCAF—the youngest one in Canada and the best. He flew the Arrow before they scrapped the program."

"I worked with a Mountie who was sent there when it happened. He thought maybe one Arrow got away. A reporter told him she heard one take off early in the morning. The noise woke her up. She said it was very distinctive. Wonder if Delbert knows anything about that. Anyway, he said it was the saddest day of his life. So much simply thrown away."

"Delbert would agree. After that, he developed and taught combat techniques which led to formation of an elite squadron known as the Pillagers. One day, when he and a student were flying their jets from Comox to Victoria, the student tried to show him up while terrain following and ended up on top of him. He had to crash land on a golf course. He would have walked away from that except a rock sticking up in the fairway knocked the plane off course and into a cliff.

"They pried him out and carried him up to a priory above the cliff. He was in a coma for days. Sylvia was there when he came out of the coma and inspired him to fight his way back."

"So that's when they met?"

"No, actually they fell in love during their high school years. Delbert has a brilliant mind. He skipped Grade twelve and went straight to university and completed a four-year engineering course in three. He lived with the Martin family. Dan Martin was and is the dean of electrical engineering. He taught Delbert to fly and the air force recruited him to be a test pilot."

"Was Sylvia with him through that?"

"No...," her expression saddened, "they were separated right up until the accident. She was a noviciate nun who happened to be at the priory when they brought him in."

"Your face tells me there's a lot more to the story, but I won't pry. It's none of my business. However, it's clear they're survivors like you. What a remarkable family."

"Strength often comes from adversity." Her mind drifted back to the murder in Vancouver. "That is, if fate leaves a path to recovery."

## Chapter 28

On Tuesday, Delbert dropped Sylvia off in Gold River for the day, eager to try his hand at some serious fire spotting. Though it was a clear, sunny day, there were reports of dry lightning strikes to the south near the mountains, a recipe for fires.

He saw no sign of smoke for over an hour. That didn't bother him. Instead, it gave him a chance to meditate like he often did when fishing. He enjoyed flying over green forests that stretched for miles. His thoughts turned back to the subject of male/female evolution. If males evolved to increase genetic diversity, surely it did not stop there. Survival of the fittest would continue to weed out bad mutations and nourish good ones. Humans had millions of years to evolve both as females and males. Over all but the last few thousand years, they were hunter/gatherers.

Given that females had pregnancies to deal with, it was clear the hunting role fell to males very early on. It made sense that males would develop characteristics advantageous for hunting. They had to be stronger, run faster, throw farther, fight harder. Their brains had to adapt to rapid strategizing and provide a fearless, aggressive attitude.

Females had to accumulate a wealth of information on what was edible, medicinal, and storable. They had to know where to find useful plants, seafood, and small creatures. And they had to work cooperatively with each other to gather the food necessary to survive hunting failures. They were the ones who decided when their nomadic clan must move on.

It made sense that male and female brains would evolve differently because of these roles. That was a generalization, of course, variations like the physical ones would still exist. He realized one could see the trend even today. Women generally approach problems differently than men. They are more likely to gather data first and work together to find solutions. Men tend to barge right into a problem and even fight for acceptance of their specific solution, regardless of its merit.

How many of his male friends would castigate him if he said that out loud? Many. Yet, the evidence was everywhere. It even explained how humanity transitioned from clans sharing territories to nations waging war. When population growth rendered the hunter/gatherer existence unsustainable, humans were forced to turn to agriculture and animal husbandry. The male role became protection of land and reproduction. Clans became cities, cities became nations.

Protecting reproduction didn't just apply to crops, flocks, and herds. It extended to females and that led to a male dominant society. Along the way, it often resulted in atrocious brutality over the past five thousand years. It still does today though females seem to be slowly regaining a balance with males, at least in major nations.

Delbert's meditation was interrupted by a wisp of smoke off in the distance. He almost missed it in the intervening haze. Increased speed gradually drew it closer. It was a fire, not a big one, but it soon would be with the moderate wind that fanned it. He tuned to the water bomber frequency.

"Delboat to Mars Base."

Mars Base. Go ahead Delboat."

"There's a side-hill fire burning two miles west of Berman Lake."

"Copy that. Two miles west of Berman Lake. On our way."

"I'll wait. Over."

"Roger."

\* \* \*

He spotted the Martin Mars flying boat lumbering toward him still about ten miles away.

"Hawaii Mars to Delboat. You still in the vicinity?"

"Roger, I have you in sight."

"Good. Stay clear. You found it while it's still a baby. I'll make two passes in the downwind direction to soak the trees in its path as well."

"Roger. I'll stay clear to the south."

"Good. I see you now. You're fine right there."

The Hawaii Mars approached from the west. The water started cascading down just before the plane reached the fire. *George was right. It is a spectacle. Like a travelling waterfall.* Within seconds, the giant plane was climbing in a turn to the north. Behind it, a mass of smoke and steam erupted. Ten minutes later it was lined up for the second pass slightly south of the first.

"Delboat, I think we got it. Any chance you could check back in an hour to be sure it's out?"

"Affirmative. I'll let the base know."

"Great. Looks like you use a lot less fuel than we would sending a chopper out."

"Roger."

"Good job spotting it when you did, by the way."

"My pleasure. I'm surprised at how quickly you returned for the second pass."

"We drank from nearby Berman Lake."

Delbert went back to the search pattern he developed. An hour later, he swung back to the fire site. He could see only one snag that still smoldered slightly. There was no brush or trees near by. He reported in and offered to check it again in the morning. They agreed it didn't warrant sending the helicopter out and thanked him for his help.

The rest of the day was uneventful. He picked up Sylvia and headed home.

* * *

Three days later, Delbert got a real introduction to fire fighting. Lightning seen out west the evening before appeared ominous. An hour after liftoff, Delbert spotted dense smoke in the distance. With southeast winds of more than twenty miles per hour reported throughout the night, the fire was obviously on the move. He immediately contacted Mars Base.

"It appears to be just east of Splendor Mountain. I'll give a better fix when I get closer."

"Roger, Delboat. We expected trouble from the weather report. Both planes are scrambling."

As he closed on the scene, Delbert could see the fire was moving rapidly through a valley. Smoke filled the sky and obscured the flames. He descended to just above the tree tops to skirt the fire line. The heat drove him a little further away.

"Hawaii Mars to Delboat. Where are you?"

"Flying along the west edge and now turning southwest."

"We can't see the terrain. We'll have to make the first pass at three thousand."

"Do you have the mountain in view?"

"Roger. We'll stay west of it and pull out to the southwest. Stay clear. Philippine Mars is ten minutes behind us."

Delbert watched the two bombers pass through the smoke. The water rained down, but Delbert wondered how much would reach the ground from that altitude. The lead pilot reported that they would reload on Buttle Lake and be back in fifteen minutes.

"Delboat. This is a bad one. We need to go in lower. To do that we need a precise course that takes us over the downwind edge of the fire. Any chance you can line us up?"

"Roger. I can fly the inbound course you need to hit the fire and carry on out the valley."

"What was your altitude at the fire level?"

"One four zero zero. You would be safe at one eight zero zero."

"Roger we'll watch for you and aim for that. We're eight minutes out."

Delbert rechecked his bearings, flew an outbound leg and turned back inbound when the water bomber came in sight.

"Delboat is on the inbound course now."

"Roger. I'm lined up, descending to one eight zero zero. Peal off to the left, Delboat. I don't want to drown you. Can you tell me when to start dumping?"

"Roger. Counting down. Five, four, three, two, one, drop."

"Hope you have us on course. Visibility is zero in here."

"You should be out in five seconds. That was a good drop."

"Daylight again! Good job, Delboat."

"On my way to pick up your partner."

He carefully set up the outbound course again and led the Philippine Mars to a run just slightly west of the first. By now there were clouds of steam mixed with the smoke. As the big planes flew off to pick up another load, he went in close to inspect the fire. It had jumped out of the wet zone in places.

"Hawaii Mars. I want to line you up outside the west edge for one pass to wet down the fire's path."

"Good idea. Lead me in."

The second pilot wanted a pass further back in the fire to see if they could cut down the smoke density. On subsequent passes, Delbert lined them up to dump strips through the fire zone. Their strategy worked. Smoke density gradually gave way to steam. Visibility improved. Buttle Lake's proximity meant they could bomb it relentlessly. The water bombers' ability to douse this large, fast-moving blaze amazed Delbert.

In a little over an hour, all that remained was a smoldering swath through the valley. Philippine Mars departed to attack another small fire reported further south. The other headed home after telling Delbert a helicopter would bring out a ground crew to mop up.

Delbert spent another two hours in his personally devised search patter combing the whole region. He found nothing and headed back to Campbell River.

# Chapter 29

Joe and Ned sat on the float after dinner. Ned had two beers with dinner and was now drinking rye whiskey. Joe glanced his way.

"You're getting into that whiskey more than usual."

"What are you, my mother now?"

"What the hell's bugging you?"

"I'll tell you what's bugging me. It's that kid you killed in Vancouver."

Joe looked around quickly to be sure no one heard. "Quiet down, goddammit. We don't know he's dead. And remember, it was us, not me."

"I saw the way his head was bent over on his shoulder. He's dead alright."

"Well, shut up about it. Someone hears you and we're both dead."

Even in Ned's big body, the whiskey began to take effect. "Now your kid brother's a killer too. There's something wrong with your family, Joe. No compassion for fellow human beings."

Joe grabbed the bottle and flung it out into the water. He grabbed the top of Ned's shirt, twisted it and pulled his face to inches in front of his own. "Listen, asshole. Those two subjects are out of bounds. You bring them up again and you'll be the next to go. That clear enough for you?"

The fierce, cold look in Joe's eyes sobered Ned.

"Yeah, that's clear. I've got to put those things out of my mind."

"You better...I'm turning in."

As he left, Joe realized Ned was now a liability. *I can't trust him to keep his mouth shut. Sooner or later he'll blab about that kid. Need to shut it permanently, make it look like an accident. Everyone knows he's dumb enough to do something stupid.*

Ned sat alone for a while and watched his half empty whiskey bottle drift slowly out into the sound. Every few minutes a small wave would splash a little water into it. As it sunk slowly, so did Ned's spirit. He wondered why he let himself get into this predicament. His only crime was being there and not able to stop it. Would a judge believe that? Not a chance after all this time without reporting it. The bottle finally sunk. Ned got up and went to bed.

* * *

"Did you have a good time last night?"

"I thought it was great. Hope Jack did too. He passed your test with flying colours."

"I'm not sure I like you calling it my test. So, he didn't bolt when you related your past problem?"

"He simply admired my survival power."

"We all do, dear."

"You're a fine one to talk. That's the garage door. Dad's home. I'll see if he needs a hand."

"He doesn't," Sylvia said to the departing daughter.

Delbert had lifted out his wheelchair, unfolded it and was about to swing onto it when Cynthia arrived.

"Can I help?"

"I'm fine." He swung onto the seat and closed the car door.

"Mum thought I would be wasting my time. Guess she was right."

Delbert laughed as he led her into the house. Sylvia wanted to know how his day went.

"I won't soon forget it. There was a bad fire over west of Buttle Lake. Out of control and moving fast. We needed both water bombers to fight it. The smoke was so dense they had to make their first pass at three thousand feet to be safe. The water just evaporated before it reached the ground in that heat.

"To make lower passes, they needed me to lead them in on the right course. They flew blind about four hundred feet over the fire. It was incredible. Those pilots are amazing. It's just as if they were flying a combat mission. They picked up water skimming Buttle Lake and dumped every fifteen minutes. I lined them up each time to gradually cover the whole fire zone. It was exciting."

"Sounds like you were in harm's way also."

"Felt like I was in the thick of battle with them, but it was safe enough."

"Safe enough to you is not necessarily safe."

Delbert shrugged. "We probably saved a hundred square miles of forest today."

Sylvia realized he would have flown through the middle of it with them if it took that to gain the feeling of accomplishment and self-worth he now enjoyed. She knew only too well how he longed for things to make his life meaningful. It wasn't easy riding a wheelchair.

"Thia was just telling me Jack passed the test with flying colours."

"Oh, wonderful! I can see you had a good time. It's written all over your face."

"One of these days I'm going to get Botox injections to keep you from reading my expressions—even if it does turn me into a psychotic monster. On second thought, cancel that."

Just the words reminded her of John. She shuddered involuntarily. Her parents remained quiet, subdued by the change in her. It wasn't hard to guess the cause.

Cynthia brightened. "Jack grew up in the Peace River area. His parents couldn't afford to send him to college, so he did what he wanted as a boy, join the RCMP. By the way, he knows a Mountie who was there when they scrapped the Arrow. He thought one was flown away that morning. Do you think it might have happened?"

Delbert forced his face to remain expressionless. "Who knows? Maybe. None has surfaced so I doubt if one ever will."

Sylvia watched him closely. She sensed that something disturbed him.

"Before I forget, there's a letter from Samantha on the kitchen table. Dan is flying up to a fishing lodge in the Queen Charlotte's the last week of this month and believe it or not, Charlie is going with him."

"Charlie—flying with Dan?" Just the thought of it made him laugh. "I'll believe it when Charlie reaches the lodge."

"Virginia and the kids will stay with her while the men are gone."

"Sounds like a therapeutic respite for both parties."

"You make it sound like they need it."

"No," he chuckled, "I didn't mean to imply that. Although I do think it's great for Charlie and Dan to spend time alone together. I've always felt Charlie's aversion to flying put a damper on their relationship."

"Do you feel guilty that Dan turned to you to fill the gap?"

"At times I felt that. I hope Charlie follows through with the flight up and back."

# Chapter 30

Back on day shift, Cynthia made the hospital rounds with Doctor Munson in the morning.

"This next patient is coughing constantly. I ordered a chest X-ray last night."

She heard the coughing as they walked through the ward entrance. Cynthia routinely reached for the chart on the foot of the bed, then stopped short. Her face turned white as she read the name that jumped out: Lawrence Adams. Munson paused, a little surprised at her expression. Then he turned to the patient.

"Good morning, I see the cough is still with us. Nurse, do we have the X-rays yet?"

"Yes, Doctor." She handed them to him. He held them up to the light.

"Cynthia, look at these."

He turned to face Cynthia. She had moved from the foot of the bed along the far side and stared at the patient who looked from one to the other.

"What's the matter?"

"He's my birth father."

The patient looked back at her, shocked.

"Cynthia?"

"Yes."

He remained confused, "You're a doctor?"

"Yes Larry."

Munson recalled her life story. *This is not good*.

"You better look at these."

She took the plates and held them up to the light. Even without proper backlighting, it was obvious lung cancer had spread through most of the left lobe. Larry's eyes remained fixed on her. His brain grappled with the astounding turn of events. Cynthia looked at Munson and nodded.

"Mister Adams," he began, to catch Larry's attention, "the pictures show that you have an extensive malignancy in the left lobe of your lung."

Larry still seemed confused.

"You have lung cancer and I'm afraid it has progressed through most of the left lobe. I need to go and study the X-rays in detail before we can recommend a course of action. Do you mind covering the rest of the rounds alone, Cynthia?"

"Yes, of course I will."

After he left, she turned back to Larry.

"Mary said she thought you were working up in Port Hardy."

Between coughs, "I was until this came up."

The old bitterness of abandonment welled up inside her, but she controlled herself out of professional discipline. His chart revealed he was only fifty-nine, too young to die of cancer. She couldn't resist a question.

"Why did you leave Mary and me?"

He was silent, except for coughs, for minutes.

"I had to leave. She stifled me. Hounded me to make more money. Then..." His voice trailed off.

"Then?"

"I caught her with another man."

She softened. "Why didn't one of you take custody of me?"

"Neither of us could afford it—and Luke was making good money. He offered to take you in."

"He did that."

She wanted to blast him with the reality of what happened but realized that would be a mean blow in his state. She wondered if he even knew Luke was dead. Emotion built in her. She fought it off and grimly thought Sylvia would be proud of her now. Sylvia was her rock. She and Delbert were her parents. This was a patient with lung cancer.

"I need to complete my rounds. We'll be back later."

He watched her go, still not fully comprehending this turn of events.

* * *

Munson looked up when she entered his office.

"It doesn't look good although it appears to be isolated to the left lobe. His best chance would be to remove it, however, we both know there's a high probability of it showing up in the right lobe before long."

"Can he withstand the operation?"

"Don't know. The odds are not too good."

"I have to bow out of this case. The decision must be yours and his. If he asks what I think, will you explain that to him?"

\* \* \*

Cynthia was still agitated when she arrived home.

Silvia took one look at her. "What's the matter, Thia?"

"My birth father is in the hospital."

"Oh, my goodness. I hope it's not serious?"

"He has lung cancer…probably terminal."

"Oh no. Did you meet with him?"

"Yes. He didn't even recognize me at first."

"Well, it's been years and he would only picture you as a teenage girl, not a doctor for sure."

"He said he left because Mary 'stifled him, hounded him' and then he caught her with another man. Neither of them could afford me and he said Luke was making big money and would take me in." She laughed sarcastically.

"Did you tell him about Luke?"

"No. I spared him that."

"That was very considerate—the right thing to do."

"You teach well."

Delbert listened to this exchange silently. Now he spoke up. "What will you recommend in the way of treatment?"

"I will not recommend. It's between Larry and his doctor. I told Doctor Munson it had to be that way. I must not be involved."

"As a doctor, that's right. Involvement as a daughter is something else."

"I'll cross that bridge when it appears."

\* \* \*

Doctor Munson called the next day and asked "Cynthia?" when she answered the phone.

"Yes."

"Munson here. I want to discuss your father's case."

"Larry's case."

"Alright. As you may know, it's very unusual to see one lobe so impacted with the other clear. I decided to take some more X-rays from various angles to recheck the right lobe. I'm sorry to say the cancer has shown up there as well. Very limited but there nevertheless."

"I see."

"Under the circumstances, an operation will not extend his life. I plan to tell him that if you agree?"

"Yes…perhaps I should join you if you don't mind."

"That would be good. Can you break away for a bit now?"

"I'll be right over."

\* \* \*

Larry could see bad news written on their faces but didn't realize how bad until the doctor predicted he had at most three months left. Cynthia stayed after Munson left.

"Is he right? I only have three months?"

"He's very knowledgeable."

"They don't have any medication for this?"

"They will drain the fluid out and give you pain medicine but there's no cure because it has spread so far and so fast."

His eyes looked teary, but he refused to cry. She also fought an emotion that caught her by surprise.

"Do you have anyone in Port Hardy who can look after you?"

"No."

"I will find a way to take care of you. They will probably want you to stay in here for a few days."

\* \* \*

"He looks suddenly old and lost. I can't abandon him the way he did me."

"I'm glad. How long will they keep him in the hospital?"

"They'll drain the lung tomorrow morning and will want to keep him in overnight at least." She hesitated, "Would it be too much of an imposition to bring him here? I could look after him in the spare bedroom downstairs."

"Correction. We can look after him."

Delbert spoke up, "He might enjoy it downstairs where he can walk out and sit on the deck. Fresh air and the ocean view may help relax him. Make the remaining days more enjoyable."

"Thank you, both of you."

# Chapter 31

Cynthia led Larry into the house two days later.

"Are you sure these folks don't mind us staying with them?"

"I live here. I'm part of their family. They want you to stay here. There's a bedroom and bathroom on the lower floor which will give you a little privacy."

"Guess I can't get used to the fact that you belong to them and not us."

"Who's us?"

"You know. Our old family."

"Our old family doesn't exist, thanks to you and Mary. I don't mean that in a bitter or accusatory sense, it's just the way it is now."

"Yeah, I have to make peace with that though I feel overwhelmed with regret at the moment."

He looked beaten down. Just the walk from car to house left him a little out of breath.

"Why don't you sit down in the front room while I take your things downstairs."

She found him crying silently when she returned.

"What's the matter? Are you in pain?"

"Pain of facing death after a useless life."

She crossed to him and put a hand on his shoulder. "I'll be here for you from now on."

"Thank you. You were a wonderful daughter growing up. You still are and I'm proud of what you've become—despite Mary and me."

"See, your life wasn't useless after all."

He managed half a smile. "Thank you."

"Rest for a while. I'll wake you for dinner if you doze off."

\* \* \*

After dinner, Larry joined Delbert on the upper deck.

"Mind if I sit a spell?"

"Please do, Larry. I like to sit out here with a cup of tea. Can I get you something?"

"No, no, I'm fine."

"Sitting here, watching life go on out there, boats running back and forth as dusk approaches is very soothing after a busy day."

"It is even without the busy day."

Delbert laughed quietly, "True enough. A busy day for me is usually more mental than physical."

"I'm very grateful for your letting me stay with you. I'm reaching the end with no one to care for me."

"Now that's not true. You have us."

"Thank you…if I become a nuisance, tell me and I'll find somewhere else."

"You're stuck with us, Larry. Besides, with a doctor and a nurse in the house, what could be better?"

"Nothing could be better, that's for sure."

They sat quietly for a while, each lost in his own thoughts.

"Delbert, can I ask you something?"

"Sure."

"It hurt me deeply when I had to give up Cynthia. I had to tell myself over and again that my brother Luke could provide for her while I could not."

"Life constantly shoves challenges our way, not all of them can be overcome."

"You seem to prove they can be overcome. But what I don't understand is how you and Sylvia came to take over custody of Cynthia. Why didn't Luke put her through medical school?"

Delbert's mind raced. *Should I tell him what happened? Does he think Luke is still alive? The truth would send him to his grave burdened with enormous guilt. I should have anticipated this problem.*

"You make it sound like you think Luke is alive?"

Shocked, "Isn't he?"

"I'm sorry to be the one to tell you. Luke has been dead for about eight years."

"Eight years? What happened to him?"

Delbert pressed on, "My folks live on Salt Spring Island. We came to know Cynthia and appreciated her fine qualities. Since we have no children of our own," he glanced down to give the impression of why, "we felt the opportunity to help Cynthia was a gift. And she has repaid us many times over."

"That's obviously a two-way street for her. You two did for her what I could never have done in my wildest dreams."

"Then we've all won out."

"Except for poor old Luke. I wonder what happened to him?"

"He died too young."

"We all die younger than we want."

"Yes, I guess most people do. I'm calling it an evening. Should I ask Cynthia to help you down the stairs?"

"I can manage. I'll come in and say goodnight to them."

* * *

After Larry had disappeared downstairs, Delbert rolled over close to Cynthia.

"Thia," he said quietly, "He asked about Luke and how you came to live with us. I told him Luke died eight years ago but not how it happened. I said we got to know you through my parents and wanted to help you, especially since we have no children of our own. He seemed to buy it; however, he will ask again what happened to Luke so we need to be prepared."

"You and Mum have always advocated facing the truth and life head on."

"Would you buy the old adage that the exception proves the rule?" He smiled sheepishly. "The truth would be a terrible load to carry to his grave."

"True. We need to spare him. If he forces the issue, let's say he was killed in the woods, and we don't know the exact details."

All three agreed that would skirt the truth the least without flagrant lies. Even so, they feared he would see through their subterfuge.

# Chapter 32

After a week and a half of nice weather free of emergencies, clouds rolled in with a vengeance. Delbert had to postpone a planned trip to a Haida village in the Queen Charlotte Islands. Sylvia decided to make some local calls in the car. With Cynthia at work, Delbert chatted with Larry and after learning he liked cards, challenged him to a game of cribbage. Just after eleven, Cynthia called.

"Dad, a woman's been mauled by a bear up in Bella Bella."

"She's still alive?"

"Barely. One of the men drove it off with a shotgun. All the planes are grounded. Could you perhaps get through under the clouds?"

"Looks like the ceiling is down to about three hundred feet here. Can she survive until morning?"

"Afraid it's doubtful based on what they described. She's badly cut up. Lost a lot of blood though they think they've got it pretty much stopped."

Delbert was silent for a minute. "Guess I can give it a shot. If I get forced down onto the water, I'll just have to taxi to the nearest shelter. Is Doctor Munson going?"

"No, he's tied up with an operation. He thinks I can handle it. Also, I can help you with navigation."

Delbert knew better than to argue with her logic. He sighed, "You'll have to pick me up here. Sylvia's off with the car."

"Be there in ten minutes."

He told Larry the plan and then decided to leave a note for Sylvia as well.

> Sylvia,
>
> Cynthia and I are flying to Bella Bella to pick up a woman mauled by a bear. If we're not back by six, it means the weather forced us to overnight along the way. Will try to get word to you.
>
> Delbert

When Cynthia picked him up, she seemed excited. He didn't share her enthusiasm. The ceiling would probably drop further as the day wore on. Their chances of making it all the way up to Bella Bella were not good, never mind returning. But he thought it worth a try since just getting a doctor to the woman would help her chances.

They took off in the river and headed up Johnstone Strait fifty feet over the water with a clear view of the shore. For forty minutes they wended their way up the narrow strait. Over the open water, the ceiling improved a little. Delbert's optimism followed suit. If they could stay in the air when they reached the narrow channel between Campbell and Denny Islands, they would at least get to Bella Bella.

Cynthia commented, "It looks like we're going to make it."

"We've got a tight stretch still ahead. Do you have their radio frequency?"

"Yes."

"Call and tell them we should be there in thirty minutes. Ask them to have someone at the dock with a flag or something to wave so we can spot them."

Their luck held as they rounded Hunter Island and entered the narrow passage. Fifteen minutes later they dropped down onto the water and taxied toward a waving flag. Two men waited.

Cynthia jumped onto the float and dragged out her emergency kit. One of the men took it and they started off up the trail. Delbert asked the other to close the door so he could turn around. Docked facing the opposite direction, he had the man tie the mooring lines and pull out the stretcher.

"Take it up. I'll wait here."

Minutes ticked by with no sign of them. Minutes he hated to waste. He knew the clouds would likely descend into fog later in the afternoon. *Cynthia, just wrap her up as best you can and get us on the way back. She knows what she's doing. I can't second guess her.* Still, he kept an eye on the trail in hopes they would appear. Finally, they came in sight, the two men carried the stretcher with Cynthia at the victim's side.

As soon as they had her loaded onboard, Cynthia started a plasma intravenous drip. The woman was unconscious. With mooring lines stowed and door closed, Delbert turned the plane around. Cynthia leaped in and they were off. The clouds were already lower than when they arrived. Delbert flew no more than ten feet off the water. Even then, wisps of clouds occasionally reached them. He felt it crucial that they get through the twisting narrow passage to open water. Otherwise, they would have to taxi back to Bella Bella with almost no visibility.

Fifteen minutes later they broke out of the narrow passage between Denny and Hunter Islands. Delbert turned south in the wider channel but cheated toward the left in hopes of seeing Namu on the way by. Staying closer to the mainland coast would help them pass inside Calvert Island. He had toyed with the possibility of avoiding these islands by flying out over the open Pacific but rejected it as too dangerous if something went wrong.

The ceiling increased slightly in this region just as it had on the northbound flight. By the time they reached the open water north of Vancouver Island, visibility allowed them to track the coastline on their left from thirty feet above the water.

"It looks like we're going to make it, Dad."

"This is the easy part. The real challenge lies ahead in Johnstone Strait."

"If we have to put into Port Hardy, I can keep her alive until tomorrow."

"I'm confident we can make it that far, probably even to Port McNeill, though it might be better to overnight at Port Hardy if it comes to that. How is she doing?"

"It's touch and go. She almost bled to death. Plasma helps. They don't prepare you in school to deal with such a bloody mess. Even if she survives, it will take a long time to put her back together again."

"We better get her through to the hospital today."

"That gives her the best chance."

"After what you saw of her, are you still glad you became a doctor?"

"More than ever." Delbert smiled.

# Chapter 33

They tracked the coastline for thirty-five minutes. At the three five zero radial from Port Hardy, Delbert turned to a heading of one five zero to head across the water in search of the Island coast. He needed to find it west of Malcolm Island in order to enter the passage leading down into Johnstone Strait. He planned to give up and divert to Port Hardy if he couldn't find it. Flight straight at a shoreline at twenty feet with limited visibility left both anxious.

The instant he spotted land, Delbert banked left to parallel the coast. Afraid of running into a point that jutted out into the sea, he moved as far from shore as possible while keeping it in sight. Thoughts of the woman perhaps dying behind him kept him pressing on. He had to dodge a small island and pass to the right of Alert Bay. Five minutes later they entered the strait.

The upper end of the strait was wide. Delbert felt more comfortable. After passing Kelsey Bay, he edged in closer to the shore to be sure he stayed below Hardwicke Island. Visibility deteriorated in the narrow strait. He was back to ten feet off the water.

"Thia, I've got to put it down before we reach the point above Rock Bay. It's too dangerous at this speed."

Delboat went from flying machine to boat. The Boston Whaler hull allowed them to taxi at about thirty knots. Delbert extended the water jet in case they had to make a quick turn.

Once they made it around the point, he set a course down the channel and lifted off again, barely skimming above the waves.

Ten minutes later he was back on the water hunting for the shoreline on his right. Clouds had become fog. Visibility so limited he had to slow down almost to a crawl. Cynthia opened her window, stuck her head out in search of the beach She heard the waves lapping on the shore before she saw it.

"Turn left. We've reached it."

Delbert left the engine idling to keep batteries charged and used the water jet to steer. Once through the tight channel, the beach took off to the right around a large bay. Delbert decided to steer a course across the bay with the intention of regaining the shore on the other side. Minutes passed slowly. Tension mounted. They should have reached it by now. He slowed until barely moving through heavy fog.

"There it is!"

Delbert swung left again and they moved slowly down the coast. They walked a tight rope between keeping contact with the shore and avoiding rocks sticking out of the water. To make matters worse, it was now late afternoon. It would soon be dusk with this cloud cover. There was one more point to get around before a straight shot into Campbell River.

"I'm going to head out into the middle of the channel, run down until we're past the point and then hunt for the beach again."

"You know best."

"Wish I could agree. Here we go."

In open water he increased the speed. When confident they were past the point regardless of tide action, he turned right to intercept the shore. Cynthia's head was out the window once more and soon she found the beach again. She kept them in contact with it while Delbert watched for rocks. It was time to announce their arrival. He called air traffic control.

"Delboat is inbound to Campbell River. Expect to arrive in twenty minutes."

"Delboat, we have no record of your IFR flight plan."

"I'm VFR, actually taxiing on the water."

"Did you say taxiing—to Campbell River?"

"Affirmative. Please contact the RCMP to meet us with an ambulance at the seaplane dock."

"Pillage, you're taking this mercy flight business too far."

Delbert laughed. "There's an unconscious woman mauled by a bear lying behind me who doesn't agree."

"We'll get them to meet you with a spotlight to guide you in."

"Thank you."

"Out of curiosity, where did you pick her up?"

"Bella Bella."

"How far have you taxied?"

"From about Browns Bay—and a couple of narrow spots before that."

"For your information, I am now shaking my head. Good luck the rest of the way."

"Thank you."

Fifteen minutes later, the shoreline led them into the river mouth. The spotlight, barely visible, became brighter as they made for it. Delbert turned on his landing lights for a moment to let them know he approached. A second light shone down on the dock to guide him in.

As soon as they tied up, medics pulled the stretcher out and started up the ramp. Cynthia slid over the aisle stand and took off after them. Sylvia came onboard.

"Apparently it's not safe to leave you alone with keys to the airplane."

"Sorry, I couldn't get word to you. Thia said it was touch and go with the woman, so we kept pushing on."

"But you can't fly in this stuff."

"It wasn't as bad farther north. We just had to taxi the last few miles."

Sylvia gave him a little hug. "I'm glad you're both safe now."

They didn't notice a reporter from the local newspaper on the float listening to them. The next edition's headline read "Ex-fighter test pilot skims waves to recue woman in Bella Bella". It's accompanying story described the adventure in graphic and reasonably accurate terms. The story was picked up and spread nationally. Two days later, Delbert received a call from his old air force commander, "Bentwing".

"Delbert, I read where you are now into hydroplaning."

Delbert laughed. "Hi Bentwing, guess it looked like that."

"You always were good at terrain following but this is taking it a little too far."

"The patient needed hospital care desperately."

"And you needed one more challenge."

# Chapter 34

By then the weather had cleared. Delbert flew Sylvia up to a Haida village on Kunghit Island at the southern tip of the Queen Charlotte Islands. It was a long flight each way which left little time for fire search or sightseeing. He wanted to stay with Sylvia in any case since the Haida people definitely did not welcome visitors.

"We can't blame them for wanting to remain isolated. In their eyes, we bring disease, often death."

"Yes. I have the thankless task of trying to convince them we bring healing and prevention also."

"You're the best candidate for the job."

"If only we could get them all immunized, it would prevent so much sickness. And now, with the new Salk vaccine we could eliminate the curse of polio."

Delbert thought back to his childhood friend Tony, struck down suddenly by polio. "Wish Salk lived twenty years earlier."

Two young men met them at the dock. The bigger one asked in broken English what they wanted.

Sylvia smiled, "I'm a public health nurse. I've come to give medical assistance to your people."

"Your people bring sickness, not take it away."

"I can give your people medicine which prevents much sickness."

After studying the strange airplane, the smaller man stared at Sylvia during this exchange. He suddenly spoke to the big one in their local dialect. A short, animated conversation followed. Then the big man turned back to them.

"Are you Sister Sylvia?"

Surprised, she responded, "Yes."

That generated a longer conversation between the men. Finally, the smaller one ran off. The bigger one said simply, "Come."

"Should I come with you?" Delbert asked.

The man interrupted, "You stay."

"I'll be fine."

Delbert was not convinced until he saw the man take her heavy kitbag to carry it to the village center. *They've heard the story of Sister Sylvia way up here already. Obviously, the west coast has its own effective communication network. She's become a legendary angel in no time at all.* He smiled. *What a woman!*

By the time Sylvia returned, Delbert had dozed off. He woke with a start when she opened the window and lowered the ramp.

"Wake up, driver. Time to head home."

She turned and thanked the big man who escorted her back. Told him they would return in two weeks to check his people again and bring more medicine. She was elated as they taxied out.

'That went well. I got every child available vaccinated and inoculated. Even many of the women. The men refused. They must view it as a sign of weakness."

"So, we return in two weeks?"

"Yes, I want to be sure there are no problems and maybe catch a few more people."

"Okay, Sister Sylvia."

She slapped him good-naturedly on the arm.

"They have exquisite carvings and artistic baskets in their lodges. They're very talented."

# Chapter 35

Jack called in the evening.

"Cynthia, hope I'm not interrupting anything."

"No, Jack, just relaxing after dinner."

"Afraid this is sort of a business call. Carson's trial is underway."

"Oh?"

"I hoped they would avoid this. The judge has granted his attorney's request to have you testify."

"When?"

"The judge will try to accommodate your schedule. His preference would be the day after tomorrow."

"Well, I'm off duty that day so I guess it's hard to say no. Will HE be in the courtroom?"

"Afraid so. They need a little testimony from me as well so we can drive down to Nanaimo together."

She brightened a little. "Thanks, I appreciate that."

\* \* \*

They met with the prosecuting attorney, Sherwood Mayne, at nine. He briefed Cynthia on what to expect.

"Carson has come up with a cockamamy story that you enjoyed erotic sex with him, and it was your idea to let him chain you to the bed while he made a quick trip into town to get you a fix, at your insistence."

"That's preposterous!"

"Of course, but we must refute it. That's why I need you to testify. The defence wants to bring out your previous record of addiction."

"I suppose the press will be in attendance?"

"Afraid that's unavoidable. The case is rather notorious."

She looked at Jack. His expression was grim.

* * *

Cynthia was called to the stand immediately after lunch recess and sworn in.

Sherwood began, "Cynthia Miriam Adams, would you please state for the court your occupation?"

"I am a medical doctor currently serving my internship at Campbell River."

"Where did you receive your medical degree?"

"At the University of British Columbia."

"Thank you. This deposition made by you has been entered as evidence. I want you to read it and tell the court under oath if it is correct and complete to the best of your knowledge."

Cynthia read the report and affirmed that it was correct.

"Thank you. No further questions at this time."

The attorney for the defence stepped forward. Cynthia instantly disliked his pompous attitude.

"Miss Adams—"

"Doctor Adams."

"Alright, **Doctor** Adams, is it true that you have been addicted to Heroin?"

"When I—"

"Just a simple yes or no, Doctor."

"Yes."

"Did you engage in prostitution?"

Shocked, she looked to Sherwood. He nodded slightly.

"Yes."

"And you resorted to prostitution to pay your way through medical school?"

"No!"

"Doctor, will you identify for the court the man you claim took you to the cabin in your deposition?"

"It was the defendant," she said pointing to Carson. Eye contact was unavoidable. Gone was his charming smile, replaced by a cold, emotionless stare designed to intimidate her. She gave him a look of hate that caused him to break contact.

"Isn't it true, Doctor, that rather than the perjury you just committed—"

"Objection, your honor. Unsubstantiated accusation."

"Sustained. There is no evidence of perjury."

"Doctor, rather than the story you related, isn't it true that you engaged in sex with the defendant in the cabin—"

"No!"

"—erotic sex and that you wanted, in fact insisted that he obtain a heroin fix for you—"

"No!"

"—to heighten the erotic experience?"

"No!"

"And in fact, asked him to leave you chained to the bed while he was gone?"

"No!"

"No further questions for this tramp, your honour."

Sherwood stepped forward again.

"I am obliged to apologize for defence's unprofessional badgering and total lack of respect, Doctor Adams. Would you please describe for the court your involvement with drugs?"

"At the end of Grade eleven, my parents separated. Neither could support me financially, so they sent me to live with my uncle Luke. They knew he could afford to look after me. What they didn't know was that his income came from drugs. I was very distraught and depressed by the loss of my friends and school life. He persuaded me that a small fix would make me feel better and showed how safe it was by doing it with me. Within a week he had me addicted.

"Then he wanted me to pay for the fixes with prostitution. I didn't want to do that and ran away to Victoria. However, the addiction drove me to seek out a pusher and before long I was a prostitute working for him. I tried to kick the habit more than once, without success.

"Later in the Fall, Delbert Pillage found me sitting between buildings in withdrawal. He and his wife Sylvia insisted I go home with them and offered to get me into a methadone treatment program. I resisted, even ran away once and almost died of an overdose. They persisted and finally succeeded in getting me cured. They also put me through college and medical school. I will forever be indebted to them. They saved my life." Her emotion showed.

"They paid for your medical education?"

"Yes, they paid for everything."

"When was the last time you used drugs?"

"When I was eighteen. Eight years ago."

"Does the availability of drugs to you as a doctor tempt you to revert to them in times of stress?"

"Never. I am completely cured. Haven't even needed Methadone for years. Incidentally, it's a misconception that addictive drugs are available to doctors. They are carefully controlled."

"Thank you. Now the defendant claims he only intended to make a quick journey to Campbell River and then return. In your testimony, you state that you walked in a circle the first day and found yourself back at the cabin. Did you find any evidence that he might have returned?"

"None. Everything was as I had left it. In fact, I scanned the cabin carefully because I was deathly afraid he would return."

"How did the defendant entice you to fly with him to the cabin?"

"He said it would be a relaxing weekend on a beautiful lake, no strings attached."

"Only chains," Sherwood snickered. "How long had you known the defendant?"

"About two weeks." She wondered why he felt this questioning necessary.

"Yet you knew him well enough to go off for a weekend alone?"

"I felt safe because we had two things in common, flying and parental abandonment."

"What did he tell you about his parents?"

"His father deserted them when he and his brother were in their early teens. His mother resorted to prostitution to support them. Then, two years ago she left them, disappeared with no further contact."

"Thank you."

Cynthia was excused.

# Chapter 36

Sherwood Mayne introduced evidence from VanIsle Airways that Carson had flown two trips the next day to transport crews to Rivers Inlet. And the following day he flew two passengers to Powell River and three to Vancouver.

Next, Jack was called. He related his conversation with Carson when they first began to search for Cynthia, how he claimed to know nothing of her whereabouts other than that he had seen her start out on a walk, obviously a red herring.

He then described his investigation of the crime scene and how he discovered two graves behind the cabin. He said the remains had been identified. There was an audible gasp in the courtroom when he announced that one was Carson's mother.

Cynthia, sitting in the gallery, understood Sherwood's strategy now. The pompous defence lawyer looked deflated as he shuffled papers in front of him. Carson stared at the floor. His flimsy case was in tatters.

Once the judge ascertained that no more witnesses were to be called, he announced that closing arguments would be heard in the morning and adjourned for the day. Sherwood beckoned Jack and Cynthia aside.

"Thanks for your help. I'm sure it was stressful for you, Cynthia, but your testimony and yours, Jack, was essential. It riddled his case and slammed the door on him."

"I hope the penitentiary door is slammed as shut," Cynthia replied.

"I fully expect it will be. You showed admirable fortitude during cross-examination, by the way. Will either of you stay for the closing tomorrow?"

"Afraid I can't. I'm on duty tomorrow." She looked at Jack.

"I need to get back too, Sherwood. We will be interested to know the verdict when it is handed down."

"Of course."

\* \* \*

Cynthia was quiet as they drove north on the Island Highway. Jack respected the privacy of her thoughts yet worried she might be brooding over the kidnapping. As they entered Qualicum Beach, she began visibly trembling. He pulled into a parking spot in front of the beach.

"Are you okay?"

"Sorry, I'm experiencing post traumatic shock. It's silly but I can't help it."

She began to cry. He put his arm around her and pulled her to him in a gentle hug.

"I'm sorry, Jack."

"Don't be. It's a natural reaction. You've been through hell."

"Thank you for arranging it so you could take me down there."

She looked up through tears at his face, then raised her hand to brush his cheek and slide behind his neck to pull them together in a kiss. A long kiss as it turned out.

"I love you. I love everything about you," he murmured.

She squeezed him into a tight embrace. The shock induced shakes transformed into excited trembling.

"I love you too." They kissed again…and again.

Finally, he half whispered, "At this rate, we may not get home before tomorrow."

She whispered in his ear, "I hope not."

\* \* \*

Jack dropped her off in time for a quick lunch before heading to the hospital. Sylvia took one look at the expression on Cynthia's face and smiled. She took hold of both hands.

"I'm so happy for you. I told you it would all work out when the right man came along."

Delbert felt a little left out. "Actually, I think I was the one who said that."

Sylvia bent over and kissed him on the forehead. "You're right, dear."

"Has he found love too, Thia?"

"Yes. I'm sure. It's real, no illusions…so natural…so great!"

# Chapter 37

On Monday morning, Cynthia received a call from Doctor Munson.

"There's been a serious injury at Rivers Inlet. From a fight apparently. They say the victim's still alive. It sounds like he needs to be brought into a hospital as soon as possible. Could you possibly take it on?"

"Sure, if you think I can handle it."

"You can. The police are trying to get an airplane capable of carrying a stretcher lined up."

"Why not use Dad's plane?"

She looked at Delbert for confirmation. He nodded.

"Can it carry a Mountie as well?"

"Yes." *I wonder if Jack will be going.*

"I'll have them call you. Thanks, Cynthia." They hung up.

"Dad, it's an injured man up at Rivers Inlet."

"Let's go."

"Do you want me along?" Sylvia asked.

"There won't be room. A Mountie must go since there was a fight involved. Dad, we need to swing by the hospital and pick up an emergency equipment kit. When the Mountie calls, tell him to meet us at the seaplane dock."

\* \* \*

Cynthia was excited to see Jack waiting for them. He reached for the heavy kit she half dragged. Within minutes they were onboard. A chop on the water slapped against the hull and made the takeoff bumpy until the wings lifted them free. The experienced pilots took it in stride. Jack remained stoic in back to conceal the modest apprehension he felt. It was an opportunity to give Cynthia news on the trial.

"Cynthia, I heard from Mayne this morning. Carson was found guilty on two counts of premeditated murder and one of attempted murder. The judge sentenced him to life."

"Did he rule out parole?"

"Very definitely. The pompous ass representing Carson tried to claim something he called psychopathic insanity. The judge agreed that the evidence showed Carson is a psychopath but there was no question that he knew exactly what he was doing. The judge said that it was because he is a psychopath and apparently incurable, Carson should never be allowed in public again."

Delbert commented, "Even Sylvia might agree there's an ultimate limit to forgiveness."

Cynthia suppressed a grin. "Thanks for the update."

A couple of hours in rough air did nothing to raise Jack's enthusiasm for flying nor did the landing at Rivers Inlet. Although sheltered, the wind up the channel managed to churn up some wave action. He told himself not to worry since the two in front remained calm and even seemed to enjoy the weather.

A man met them at the dock. Cynthia and Jack leaped out. Jack grabbed the kit. Cynthia raised the ramp and dropped the top half of the door. Delbert swung the plane around and the two on the dock tied off the mooring lines. They followed their guide up the road. Delbert was left to either wait or make his way up the dirt road.

While Jack asked witnesses for an account of the incident, Cynthia began work on the victim. His vital signs were not good, a slow, weak pulse, low blood pressure and below normal body temperature. A bullet had entered his forehead and exited through the top of his skull. Not much she could do there other than stop any bleeding, try to drain any local blood in the brain cavity and keep the area clean.

A second bullet had entered his left side and exited out the back. That could be serious if it punctured the intestinal tract. However, it was the third hole that concerned her most. There was no exit wound. The bullet must still be lodged in the lower part of his chest. But if it glanced off a rib, it could be anywhere. If it damaged an artery, he couldn't be moved until the bullet was removed and the artery repaired.

*Am I qualified to perform this operation? There's no alternative. What if I botch it and kill him? Calm down, Cynthia. You were trained to handle unexpected emergencies.* She was cutting clothing away from the wound as she weighed the situation. That action alone committed her to continue. The head wound must have rendered him unconscious. She realized his vital signs made an anesthetic both impossible and probably unnecessary.

Jack glanced at her from time to time as he listened to a witness. She retrieved surgical implements from the kit and began to prod delicately while visualizing the anatomy that lay below. A lateral incision allowed her to penetrate further. She slowly worked her way along the apparent bullet path widening the opening as she went and stemming bleeding as much as possible. Finally, she tapped what sounded like metal. The bullet was flattened against a rib in back.

Although there was no crucial damage, it had grazed an artery leaving it weakened and slightly oozing blood. His low blood pressure had prevented it from rupturing. It was too fragile to leave untreated. Fifteen painstaking minutes later, she felt it was safely repaired. The next step involved removing the bullet, carefully preventing it from touching the artery and damaging other blood vessels. More time was needed to control bleeding and suture her way out.

She handed the bullet to Jack. "Do you need this for evidence?"

"Thank you. I couldn't help admiring your artistry with a knife."

"We prefer to call them scalpels," she said with a short laugh.

She turned her attention to the wound in his side. Surgery in this area was less sensitive and proceeded quickly. The bullet had nicked his colon. Repair could be put off until he was in a hospital. She taped the colon to temporarily seal it and prevent any infection. Returning to the head wound, she inspected the holes in his scalp as best she could. There was no significant blood flow within the skull. She temporarily plugged the holes in the bone and dressed the outer skin surface to prevent further blood loss and keep the area sterile.

"He's ready to transport."

"I'll get the stretcher."

Jack ran back to the dock. Delbert had the stretcher out ready for him.

"How is he?"

"Cynthia worked on him for a while and says he's now ready to move. He's unconscious and looks to have lost a lot of blood."

As the locals watched, Jack and Cynthia loaded him onto the stretcher. One of them offered to help Jack carry him down to the dock. Another carried the emergency kit.

As they walked, Cynthia asked, "Do you have what you need?"

"The shooter was a rough young character named Bobby Deshane. He's taken off into the woods. I'll have to come back with King and track him down."

"Perhaps Dad can bring you back after we drop this one off."

Delbert rolled onto the airplane ahead of them and helped guide the stretcher loading process. With it locked in place, he swung the plane around for them to board. Cynthia wanted the rear seat so she could tend to the patient. In minutes, she had an intravenous drip attached and was giving him blood plasma before they taxied out.

The takeoff was not as bumpy as in Campbell River but the flight was still rough. Delbert could tell Tony's spring system was a very worthwhile addition. Cynthia monitored the victim's condition and gave him an injection designed to invigorate his heart. His vital signs improved as the trip ground on. Up front, Jack found flight more relaxing than he had in the back seat. An ambulance waited for them in Campbell River. Cynthia rode with it to the hospital.

# Chapter 38

"Cynthia said you might fly King and me back up there."

"Sure. Whenever you're ready."

"That's a lot of flying in one day."

"Not for me."

"Okay, I'll get the dog."

He was back in twenty minutes with King and a box of sandwiches, cookies and milk.

"You must be hungry if not tired."

"The thought of eating has crossed my mind."

King seemed to have grown attached to Delboat, even eager to jump onboard and glad to see Delbert again. With Jack in the front seat, they were soon airborne. The winds were a little calmer, the air a little smoother this time. The two men ate lunch and chatted while King surveyed the unfolding scenery.

"I gather the patient will survive?"

"Cynthia thinks so though it's hard to assess the brain damage. She did an amazing job up there. She's very talented. I'm a hog looking at a wristwatch when it comes to surgery, but I'm convinced she had some very delicate work to perform."

"She has accomplished so much, it's hard to be surprised when she performs some new feat."

"You must be very proud of her."

"She makes us proud."

"There seems to be a mutual admiration between the three of you."

Delbert laughed, "I guess so."

"Perhaps I shouldn't say this but I hope there's room for a fourth."

"It's not a closed club."

They were silent for a few minutes. Jack was in a quandary.

"Perhaps it's unfair to prevail on you, Delbert, but I would value your opinion on something."

"Let's find out if it's fair or not."

"I'm shocked by how quickly a very strong attachment to a person can develop. As you probably have guessed, that's happened with my feelings toward Cynthia."

"I hope you are not going to ask me how she feels about you."

"No, she's made that pretty clear. I think she reciprocates my desire to spend as much time together as humanly possible. That's not the concern."

"Oh?"

"Even though we've known each other only a short time, I have an urge to ask her to marry me. Trouble is, the rational side of me asks how I can subject her to my life style, my career."

"You're afraid you will leave her widowed?"

Jack laughed weakly, "I suppose that should be a concern. Cynthia's embarking on a promising career as a doctor who will benefit thousands of patients. Every few years, I get transferred to a new location. Is it fair to disrupt her career that way? And perhaps to raise a family?"

Delbert stared silently out the front for a moment.

"I need to share a little family history which you must keep in confidence."

"Of course."

"I skipped the final year of high school and went to university. During the next summer, the Air Force sent me back to pilot training in Ontario. Sylvia finished high school and took a summer job with the intention of coming to Vancouver in the Fall."

Delbert paused before continuing, "Her boss raped her and when she found herself pregnant, in desperation she tried to perform an abortion on herself. It robbed her of the ability to carry a baby. She decided it wouldn't be fair to deprive me of children, so she buried herself in a convent to force me to look for another mate."

Jack tried to ignore the tear in Delbert's eye.

"I searched for her for years without success. Then the crash brought us together again. Only this time I was the one who felt she should not be burdened with looking after half a man. I told her that when she proposed to me."

"She proposed?"

"Yes. She said over the years she came to realize it is wrong to make other people's decisions for them. She said when a person proposes marriage, he—or she—has decided. All that remains is for the other to accept or decline. My heart overruled my brain and I have been thankful ever since."

Jack responded quietly, "Thank you, Delbert."

Both men were silent, not knowing exactly what to say next. Delbert decided to move on to another subject.

"How do you plan to proceed at Rivers Inlet?"

"If Deshane hasn't returned to the settlement, King and I will track him down."

"Isn't that dangerous if he's a skilled woodsman?"

"It calls for caution, but King will sniff him out and warn me when we get close. Most criminals think twice before taking a shot at a Mountie."

"I hope you don't count on that."

Jack laughed, "No, it's more of a windfall."

After they landed and Jack and King disembarked, Delbert asked if he wanted him to wait for them.

"It might take half an hour or many days to catch him."

"I'll stay for two hours. If you don't show, I'll head home and wait for your call."

"Can you pick up my walkie talkie on your radio?"

"Sure. Let me see what band you use."

He studied the device. "I can pick that up. Call me and let me know what you find up there."

Delbert settled into meditation as he watched Jack and King head off up the road. *I like him. He's a solid character, good for Cynthia just as she would be good for him. I hope they unite. It would bring closure to her. She would be a delight for any man who spends time with her.* He tuned one radio to Jack's frequency. Half an hour went by.

"McCain to Delboat."

"I read you, Jack. What's the situation?"

"He hasn't shown. People here think he's in the valley to the east. King has a scent to follow so we'll head up that way."

"Maybe I'll take a spin around the area. See if I can spot him for you. He won't hear me."

"Okay. Be careful. He may have a rifle."

Delbert climbed to five thousand feet. It would be difficult to spot the silent plane. Even if discovered, the chance of hitting him with a rifle was remote. The valley looked desolate. On a pass back toward the settlement, he saw Jack and King heading around a ridge leading north instead of east. *I bet they hoped to send him on a wild goose chase to protect their friend.*

He flew on by them to search the new area. Another small valley opened to the north west. Part way over it he noticed a small cabin, just a shack nestled in the trees. He called Jack and reported its location. It seemed prudent to circle the area in search of other buildings. He found none. As he passed the shack again, a man came out and urinated. Delbert turned to stay behind him and head away. When he reported back to Jack, they agreed it was probably his man. He would approach with caution.

On the ground, King growled softly when they entered the small valley. Their target was near. Once he had the shack in sight, he signalled King to flank it on the right.

He called out in a loud voice, "Bobby Deshane, this is the RCMP. Come out with your hands up."

No answer.

"We know you are in there. We saw you. Your victim is alive. Don't make things worse by resisting arrest."

He waited patiently for his words to sink in. Delbert circled overhead. After five minutes, the door opened and Bobby emerged, his hands up to his shoulders. Jack came forward slowly. Suddenly, Bobby reached behind him and drew a revolver. As his arm came up, a blur from his left was all he saw before King's teeth bit into his wrist and dragged him down. A gunshot sent a bullet off into the woods. The bite tightened until the hand let go of the pistol.

Jack reached them and kicked the gun away, called off King, flipped Bobby face down and cuffed him. He stood up and called Delbert to let him know they would meet him back at the dock. After retrieving the pistol for evidence, he nudged Bobby along the path. It took half an hour to walk out. The locals were silent when the two men and dog appeared.

"I will ignore the real possibility that you tried to send me in the wrong direction. King made it a futile charade. However, you might think about the wisdom of abetting a criminal and reconsider your loyalty to a man that might just as easily have turned on any of you."

On the dock, Delbert had the ramp down for King to enter. He then turned the airplane around. Jack made Bobby sit in the rear seat, fastened his seatbelt, then took one of the mooring ropes and tied his feet and body to the seat. They headed back to Campbell River.

* * *

Delbert arrived home just before nine.

"You must be starved."

"Is there something I can snack on?"

"I'll reheat your dinner."

"Thanks. Quite an adventure today, medical emergency mission and a manhunt. Is Cynthia still at the hospital?"

"Yes, she called to say she wanted to assist the operation on the man. She said it presented a good learning experience."

"Jack told me she performed some very delicate surgery before he could be moved. Her composure impressed him."

"He will learn she never stops being impressive."

"I think he already has. They make a good couple."

"Don't jump to conclusions, let things evolve."

"Evolve or gestate?"

She laughed. "I suppose you could call growing love a gestation."

"Jack's a fine man. Always seems to be in control when needed. Guess that was part of his training. The chase and arrest was exciting."

"What? Were you there?"

"Sort of—I was right overhead."

"In danger?"

"Not really."

She gave a searching look. "Don't tell me your next step will be to mount a machine gun on Delboat."

"I plan to stay out of range instead. Had my fill of bullets back at Musgrave's Landing. It is interesting how much has happened to us in the short time we've been here. I thought Campbell River might seem dull after Victoria. It's anything but. With your adventures, forest fires, mercy flights and manhunts, I wonder what will come next."

# Chapter 39

Charlie hooked the gaff through the salmon's lower jaw and lifted it with the handle over his shoulder to carry it into the lodge.

"My first Tyee. Must be at least forty-five pounds."

"Forty at least," Dan agreed.

"Makes the flight in and out worthwhile."

Dan smiled as he lifted the two smaller salmon with the net and led them up the ramp. They had caught fish each of the four days but this was the first Tyee. What a thrill when it first leaped out of the water. It took Charlie over thirty minutes to land the big fish. They would be carrying a lot of salmon home, some smoked, most frozen and wrapped in ice.

"You packed and ready to go? Wheels up before three."

"Floats up. I'll be there."

\* \* \*

Dan completed his pre-flight checklist.

"According to the charts, our weight is well within limits but it's the heaviest load I've lifted off with so far."

"Way to fill me with confidence."

Dan advanced the power. They began the takeoff run. It seemed to go on forever before they lifted off.

During climb out, Dan suggested, "Let's swing a little east and go by Mount Waddington, then down over Whistler."

"You're the captain. Isn't Waddington the highest mountain in Canada?"

"No, that's Mount Logan in the Yukon. It's the highest peak totally within B.C. although if you count the half of Mount Fairweather in B.C., it's higher also."

"This whole coast provides magnificent scenery, but it looks damn rugged when you get away from the water."

"Yeah. The old float plane jockeys used to say stay within gliding distance of water."

"And you want to head into the mountains."

Dan laughed. "We'll be safe."

An hour later, they were closing on the mountains to their left. Dan climbed to nine thousand feet which was as high as he wanted to go without oxygen and probably about all they could do with floats attached anyway. He planned to skirt the mountains on the west side keeping a clear exit route down to the coast.

The mountains were spectacular. Even Charlie forgot his fear of flying and tendency to become nauseated. Dan was the first to notice the airplane slowing to maintain altitude. A glance at the wing leading edge shocked him. Ice was building fast. He turned west and began to descend rapidly. He had witnessed icing before but nothing like this.

He levelled off at five thousand. Terrain ruled out going lower until he could get closer to the coast. The airplane didn't know that. The ice was weighing them down — destroying the wing's lift.

"What's the matter?" Charlie half yelled.

"We've got serious ice. Look for a lake just in case."

"Can't see anything."

Now Charlie knew why he was right to fear flying. He would gladly give the Tyee back to the sea if this trip would just become a dream—or even a nightmare. Only Dan realized how desperate their situation had become. He dialed the emergency frequency and began to transmit.

"Mayday! Mayday! Cessna Charlie Hotel One Seven One Niner—"

He was interrupted by the need to control with both hands. They were losing altitude rapidly. He dodged between hills. A small lake appeared dead ahead. Too small. He had no choice. He pulled back power to hit the near edge. The floats slammed into the water, hydroplaned across the lake, hit the far beach, and slid up into the trees. Both men were unconscious.

# Chapter 40

Joe noticed Ned became edgier each day, a time bomb that could go off without warning. He had to be silenced. Half the crew now worked toward the next campsite. Joe and Ned were falling timber over half a mile in the opposite direction, alone much of the shift. That provided the opening Joe needed.

Ned was working a gulley just beyond a ridge. Joe watched from behind some brush as Ned trimmed a fallen tree. He had a three-foot thick branch to use as a club. Ned finished the log, wiped his brow and moved on to the next tree. He sized it up and began the wedge cut. With the chain saw noise, Joe could walk right up to him and club him across the back of the head. Ned went down.

Joe dragged him about twenty feet from the trunk, took Ned's saw and began changing the cut. Joe's expertise allowed him to fall the tree precisely on top of Ned despite a side lean. He moved around to be sure Ned was dead and was surprised to find him staring back with accusing eyes. Pinned as he was, the weight of the tree prevented breathing. Joe sat and watched him slowly die. Then he gave a little laugh, recut the stump to make sure everything said it was an accident and went back over the ridge.

After cutting and trimming another tree, he put his saw down and climbed over the ridge, cleared away branches to get to Ned, bucked the tree on either side of him with Ned's saw and pulled his body out. Then he ran back to camp shouting for help. The run left him panting just as he planned. Loggers came running.

"Ned felled a tree on himself. I got him out but he's dead."

A gang took off after him. There was no question Ned was dead. They carried him out. When Delbert and Cynthia responded to their radio call, Cynthia checked the body and officially pronounced him deceased. They loaded him on the stretcher and flew him back to Campbell River.

\* \* \*

Sylvia met them at the ramp, distraught.

"Something happened to Dan and Charlie. They haven't made it back to Vancouver."

"Maybe they're still at Langara."

"No. They left there at three this afternoon. Samantha called them."

"It's almost eight now. They could still be flying or maybe they had to land somewhere along the coast."

"I don't like the feel of it. They would have radioed a change in plans."

"You're right. I'll see if air traffic control knows anything."

He rolled back onboard and radioed ATC and identified himself.

"I have friends who are overdue on a flight from Langara to Vancouver in a Cessna one eighty-five float plane. Do you have any info on their status?"

"Do you have their tail number or pilot in command name?"

"No tail number. Pilot is Dan Martin."

"Roger. We had a Mayday call from him at sixteen twenty-seven. It was interrupted before he could give his location or problem. We have search planes on his route but no emergency beacon signal yet."

"Thank you. Please keep me advised. I can act as a go-between with their families."

"Will do, Delboat."

He gave ATC his home phone number, then passed the ominous news to the two women on the ramp. They gasped.

"Dan is such a meticulous pilot. I can't imagine him putting them in danger."

"What can we do?"

"There's not enough daylight left to get up there and join the search. If we don't hear anything tonight, we'll fly up first thing in the morning."

He asked the dock attendant to refuel the plane and they drove home.

* * *

All three spent a fitful night. There were no phone calls other than a tearful one with Samantha and Virginia. They arrived back at the dock an hour before dawn. When the sky lightened, they were on the direct flight path between Langara and Vancouver, heading north. ATC informed them that no sign of the airplane had been found.

If Dan had departed exactly at three, he would have flown an hour and a half before the Mayday call. No one could tell them exactly when the airplane took off so they would have to search most of the way to Langara. On the other hand, much of the last half of the flight path could be ignored.

Nothing turned up on the northbound flight as they suspected. Delbert turned and flew a parallel path five mile left back down. He scanned the water for oil slicks with little hope for success. *A regular search pattern is useless. Others are doing that already.* Instead, he decided to go down lower and fly up and down each inlet and over the coastal lakes.

By late afternoon, he felt he had covered all of them. No sign of Dan. Discouraged and much afraid, they returned to Campbell River. All four women were crying after the phone call reporting in. Delbert felt emotional stress too. *What could have happened? If he crashed into the water, they might have sunk without a trace. Not likely. Something would have floated up. Usually the floats appear upside down in the water.*

He pulled out both the air navigation chart and an atlas after dinner. While the chart gave terrain elevations, he wanted to see the big picture of mountains, inlets and sea. *What would Dan think about for the flight home? They probably enjoyed the time together at Langara. Charlie probably dreaded the flight back. Dan would want to take his mind off it.* The atlas showed clearly the line of high mountain peaks to the left of their flight path. *Dan might have chosen to fly more in their vicinity rather than the straight line just to distract Charlie. I doubt if that area has had more than a cursory pass to try and pick up his emergency beacon signal. I hope he didn't go that way. If he got in trouble, there might not be a way out. That's the logical place to look next anyway.*

# Chapter 41

Charlie slowly regained consciousness just before dusk. His head and legs ached. Pinned in his seat, the only thing he could move was his head and left arm. His father was not moving. He couldn't tell if he was breathing.

"Dad. Dad!"

No response. With mounting fear, he forced his hand to check for a pulse on Dan's carotid artery. It felt weak and slow.

"Hang on, Dad. They'll find us. Keep fighting. Please!"

He looked around, tried to understand their situation. The airplane was up against a giant cedar trunk which had driven the engine back into him. A large branch ran along his side of the airplane. It would prevent him from opening the door. Another branch had broken the windshield on Dan's side and obviously hit his head. A lot of bleeding that seemed to have stopped. All he could see in every direction was cedar tree. He began to wonder how much of the airplane would be visible from the air.

Every few minutes, he checked on Dan. Implored him to wake up. When he finally remembered the radio, he experienced a flash of optimism that was dashed when he identified the mangled units. It turned dark quickly when the sun dropped below the mountains to the west. Temperature dropped rapidly. He started to shiver. *How can Dad survive this?* There was nothing he could do to combat the cold. He fought to stay awake for almost two hours, then drifted off into something between sleep and unconsciousness.

He woke again when sunlight filtered through the tree. It took determination to feel for Dan's pulse. His body felt cold but the feeble pulse persisted. Midway through the morning, he heard branches moving on Dan's side. *They've come!* He looked over. A bear stared in the window. It clawed at the door and window. Charlie yelled at it. Unable to get in, it finally left.

*They must find us today.* But as the day wore on, he neither saw nor heard anything else. He thought often of Virginia and the kids. They would be frantic by now. *I will stay alive as long as it takes searchers to find us and take us back to them.* But by evening, he couldn't help wondering if they would survive another night.

Fatigue made sleep inevitable despite the freezing temperature. He woke slowly in the morning. The cold enticed him to simply continue to sleep. He recognized it and fought his way awake. He hesitated a long time before feeling for Dan's pulse. There still was one, weaker and slower than yesterday.

"Hang on, Dad. They'll find us today for sure." He wished he could believe that.

*  *  *

Cynthia couldn't join them in the morning due to her work schedule. Delbert and Sylvia set off to the north on the east side of the direct flight path. It was a clear day, visibility unlimited. Yet, they saw no sign of the plane. Delbert turned further east for the southbound run. To fly closer to the mountains, he had to climb and managed to reach seven thousand feet.

Sylvia periodically interrupted her search to gaze at the nearby mountains.

"They're magnificent!"

"What?"

"The mountains."

"And dangerous. There's a little icing. Fortunately, the engine exhaust along the leading edge keeps it from building. If it starts accumulating on the fan blades, we'll have to go down to warmer air."

"Could that have happened to Dan?"

"It shouldn't have. With all his experience, he must have run into ice and flown out of it. Still—it can happen quite suddenly. An escape route is essential. In areas like this, that can be a problem."

"Are you saying he might have crashed in here?"

"No, but he may have had to ditch in one of these mountain lakes."

Sylvia decided it was time for another of the many prayers she had offered in the last couple of days. Delbert scanned the terrain with particular attention paid to lakes. Once, he spotted a small lake beyond a knoll to his left and circled back to check it out. Nothing. Perhaps his speculation was faulty. He tried not to visualize Dan and Charlie buried in crash wreckage.

To focus on the search, he tried to picture how Dan would have flown down below him with a load of ice. It kept him from brooding. He could safely descend to five thousand now. Dan would be flying between the ridges to get to that next valley to the sea. If I was too low to make that valley, I would put it down on any piece of water, even that one. "Sylvia, look!"

"Where?"

"That little lake."

"I don't see anything."

"Skid marks on the far side." He forgot to make allowance for his unusually strong vision.

"I see them now but there's no airplane."

"It must be buried in those cedars. I just caught a glimpse of it. We've found them!"

He was on the radio to the air traffic center advising them of his location and belief that he had found an airplane down, probably theirs.

"I am on Port Hardy Radial Zero One One and Malcolm Radial Three Four Niner. It is on the east edge of a very small lake, not much more than a widening in the river, buried in trees with float skid marks from the beach. Very rugged terrain."

"Roger. Copy that."

They repeated the radials for confirmation and said a rescue party would be sent in. Delbert didn't hear a sense of urgency in the transmission and couldn't tell if they assumed it was too late to expect survivors or the normal forced calm in all radio communications.

"Sylvia, I need your opinion."

"On what?"

"It's been two days; however, they may still be alive. Don't know how long it will take to get a rescue party in. We can land on that puddle but not take off from it. There's a possibility we can taxi down the river to where it widens into a lake. On the other hand, we might be too late, and we might be stuck there until they rescue us. Should we take a chance and go down?"

"Yes," she said immediately.

"Okay." He circled back around and approached with full flaps as close to stall speed as he dared. Immediately after he hit the water, he cut the engine, flipped the water jet around and applied full power to the pump. The far beach became near in a hurry. He rotated the water jet enough to put them into a skidding turn that brought them parallel to the beach barely in time. When the speed bled off enough to safely taxi, he turned back toward the skid marks.

Sylvia started to breathe again. "That was close—too close according to my beating heart."

Near the beach, Sylvia dropped her door to platform level and scrambled ashore. She pushed her way through cedar branches as best she could and finally caught a glimpse of Charlie. *Did his head move? I think so.* The branches were too thick to get closer. Perhaps she would have better luck on the other side.

"It's them." she called to Delbert. "I can't reach Charlie. I'll try the other side."

## Chapter 42

Charlie dreamed he heard a voice, which roused him from his stupor. He became aware of branches rustling on Dan's side. *The bear is back.* He turned his head to shout at it. Sylvia's face was at the window, framed in cedar bows. *I'm hallucinating.* She was prying open the window.

"Charlie, speak to me."

"Sylvia." It was not much more than a rasping whisper.

She was frantically trying to open the door, breaking off small bows, bending others. Finally, it was open enough to squeeze her head and shoulders in. Her first instinct to check for a heartbeat on Dan's neck scared her until she detected the faint, slow pulse.

"You look pinned in."

He nodded yes.

"I can't get to your door. I'll have to pull Dan out first, then you."

He nodded again. His left hand reached over to unbuckle Dan. Sylvia reached in around the bottom of Dan's seat, found the latch and pulled the seat back on its tracks as far as she could. Her heart pounded as she grabbed him by the armpits and pulled. His limp body followed her out through the branches. His head wound started to bleed again. Sylvia ran to the airplane for bandages.

"They're both alive. Charlie is pinned in his seat weak but conscious. Dan's in a coma, barely alive."

"I'll turn the plane and get the stretcher out."

Dan's forehead was bandaged when he dropped his ramp and rolled back to pass out the stretcher. Sylvia put it on the bank next to Dan and lifted his upper body on. A movement caught Delbert's eye. A grizzly was wading along the shore toward them. He spun around, pulled out the flare pistol, rammed in a cartridge, aimed, and fired. The flare bounced off its back and burst into flame.

Distracted and angered by the flare, it stood up on its hind paws and roared. Sylvia saw it for the first time and screamed. Delbert reloaded, took careful aim, and fired again. This one hit it in the chest and stuck to the fur. When it flashed into flame, the bear howled and tried to beat it off its chest. Even though the flare fell sputtering in the water, its fur still burned. It turned and ran back into the woods.

"We need to work fast."

Sylvia had Dan loaded on the stretcher. She waded out to hand the head end to Delbert. With one on each end, they lifted him. Delbert put his end on his lap and rolled back toward the front. Once the stretcher was in place, Sylvia locked it down and headed back for Charlie. Delbert raised the ramp and turned the airplane around.

Sylvia had to squeeze her way entirely into the airplane this time. For the first time, she noticed the stench of rotting fish. *That's what brought the bear. Need to hurry before it or another one comes.* Charlie looked hopelessly jammed in.

"I need to get your seat back."

"If you can't get me out…take Dad to a hospital."

"Be quiet. We'll get you out."

She crawled over his shoulder trying to reach the seat latch. Everything felt scrunched together. His legs were almost certainly broken. He groaned when she forced her hand in behind the left one. There was a bar that felt like a seat latch. She pulled. Nothing. She pulled with panic fed adrenalin. There was a rasping click and the seat came free. She wormed her way back a little and pulled the seat to the end of its track. Charlie winced in pain as nerves began transmitting again.

"I've got to pull you out this side. Can you help?"

"Only my left arm works."

"Hang on. This will hurt."

Sylvia decided there was no alternative but to pull him out by brute force. He howled in pain as feet came free when she dragged him across. She had to roll him on his side to get him through the narrow door opening. He couldn't suppress another scream when his broken legs came through.

"I'm sorry, but we have to get out of here before another bear shows up."

She dragged him to the beach. He fainted from the pain. Delbert had the plane ready. He wondered how they would get Charlie into his seat through the still open door.

"I'm going to put him in the front seat so I can tend to Dan."

"I can't help you."

How many thousand times had he felt useless? Never so much as now. He stared in shocked as Sylvia lifted Charlie, one arm under his legs, the other across his back and waded out with him as though carrying a giant baby. She stepped up on the ramp and lowered him into the seat. Delbert reached over to help buckle him in.

Sylvia retrieved a splint and bandages from their medical supplies. She placed the splint between his lower legs and bandaged them together as gently as possible. Delbert watched, periodically scanning outside. A second grizzly appeared.

"There's another bear. Get in. Quick!"

She leaped into her seat and pulled up the ramp. Delbert was already backing out into the lake. The bear came after them, then suddenly stopped, looked from them to the trees and turned in that direction.

"They smell the rotting fish."

"Better my Tyee than rotting pilots." Dan was awake again.

Delbert chided him, "I suppose that fish will gain twenty pounds now that we can't verify its weight."

"How did you find us?"

"Just asked myself what two nutty fishermen would do?"

Charlie chuckled through his pain. Once they were out in the middle of the lake, Delbert paused to review their situation. He glanced back. Sylvia had an intravenous needle in Dan's arm and a second needle attached to the other end of the tube. She stuck it into her elbow. He could see blood flow through the tube.

"What are you doing?"

"He needs blood."

"Don't give too much, Wonder Woman."

She laughed. He worried. How could she tell how much she donated? Her face turned white. She fainted. He lurched over and yanked the tube and needle out of her arm. *Damn it, she gave too much. Wake up, Sylvia. We need you.* Within five minutes she stirred, regained consciousness, stared down at the tube and reached for it.

"Don't you dare stick that back in your arm!"

She smiled weakly, "I'm going to connect him to a bag of serum now."

"Is he still alive?"

"Yes. Barely. We need to get him to a hospital soon."

Her thoughts turned back to Charlie. She dug out a bottle of water and two chocolate bars.

"You must be parched and starved. Here. Drink slowly."

"Thanks. I need that. Don't know if you noticed but pinned in I had to wet and crap my pants."

"Yes, afraid I did as soon as we got away from the fish smell. You had no choice."

Delbert weighed in. "It's pretty obvious even now. I'll remind you of it about every five years. Even tell you how hard it will be to get the seat clean and odor-free again."

# Chapter 43

Another grizzly appeared headed for the downed airplane. Bigger even than the first, it lumbered into the cedars. Roar after roar resounded across the water. The smaller one slid back out, blood flowing from its shoulder. It was followed by the big one who stood on its rear paws. It bellowed. The younger one rolled over, stood up and slinked off. Majesty and savagery on a grand scale. Despite their predicament, they gazed in awe at the spectacle.

Delbert broke the silence. "I don't believe we belong here."

"Can we try the river? We need to get them both to a hospital."

"That's our best alternative. All we need is a long enough straight stretch to get off."

Charlie showed a slowly returning spirit. "I'd prefer you just taxi all the way."

Delbert shook his head, started the engine to recharge batteries and steered for the river exit. The riverbed was flat but constantly winding. They had no trouble navigating at first. A quarter of a mile on, it began to shallow. With his window open, Delbert could hear the water flow ahead. He slowed to a crawl.

"We may be approaching rapids."

Round the next bend there was a straight stretch of shallow water running quickly. A few rocks penetrated the surface. It looked like he could drift between them without the water jet to steer the plane. They would probably hit rocks on the bottom, but all were worn smooth by the river. The big question was what lay beyond. A waterfall would force them to beach the plane. He could see a short stretch of calm water below the rapids.

"This is a point of no return. I think we can negotiate this stretch but there's no way of getting back up if we run into a worse obstruction later."

"You said the rescue party would rescue us if we are stranded," she reminded him.

"Okay. Here we go."

He studied the water flow to determine the best entry point. When he reached it, he retracted the water jet and let the plane drift. It picked up speed. They felt it bump on rocks. One of the large rocks passed too close for comfort. Moments later the plane sideswiped another. A few more bumps and they slid out into calm water. Delbert quickly extended the water jet to bring the plane under control.

Charlie asked, "Do you think they punctured the hull?"

"I doubt it. Even if one did, it's filled with Styrofoam. It will still keep us afloat."

Delbert hoped for a straight stretch as he continued down. That was until he found one. It presented a new problem. The river was hemmed in by rock walls on either side. Even though the river looked deeper, water flowed faster through the narrow passage. Delbert brought the plane to a stop. The gap was clearly narrower than his wingspan. They were trapped.

Present a problem to a creative person and he or she will find a solution. Delbert believed in that, lived by it in fact. He also believed the solution was often both simple and staring one in the face. Still, it took him a while to stumble onto it.

"Our wingspan is too great for the gap. We need to turn sideways."

"What?"

"If we turn the airplane sideways it will slip through."

He knew it would be tricky to keep the airplane positioned in the currents but it seemed manageable. He started it into the current, then swung it around to face the right cliff. With the nose three feet from the rock, he rapidly maneuvered the water jet to maintain wing clearance. If one wingtip hit rock and slammed the airplane around, they would be wedged in the gorge. Sudden, it didn't seem as brilliant a solution. There were a couple of near misses before they drifted out into a wider stretch.

"Sorry, that was foolhardier than I anticipated."

"We made it."

"Yes. I hope we don't face another stretch like that."

They taxied on. Then, rounding a bend they encountered a lake on the left. The river exited not far from where it entered. The lake itself was set in a valley with hills on three sides. It was long enough for the takeoff run. However, he would have to bank after liftoff and fly a circle around to the river exit. There was scant margin for error.

Delbert taxied to the far end. He wondered if he could lift off in time from this direction to turn out through the river exit.

"Just so you know, this is a test. I'm not taking off."

He advanced power to begin a takeoff run. Before he reached sixty knots, he pulled it back again and used the water jet to slow down. The easy way out didn't work. He would have to takeoff in the other direction and fly the circle route.

"I wish that river exit was at one end or the other but it's not. How is Dan?"

"The blood and serum seems to have stopped the decline for now. He needs real medical care badly."

Delbert decided the takeoff risk was manageable and under the circumstances warranted. He started the takeoff run facing almost in the opposite direction to gain what speed he could and still turn back on course. Once turned, he applied full power to the fans and left the water jet adding what it could. As usual the airplane accelerated smoothly and quickly though the lake ahead was shrinking rapidly. Finally, at sixty knots he pulled the nose up. He needed to gain enough height to prevent a wingtip touching the water. Trees were coming up fast. He began the bank as it climbed keeping the wingtip just a few feet off the water.

The steep banked turn pressed all three into their seats. Both passengers looked fearfully at the water rushing by, expecting to crash into it or trees at any moment. Neither said anything. Neither breathed. Delbert eased off the bank angle along the back side of the lake as much as the shoreline permitted. Lift generated by the wings to hold the turn was now shared with climb. A more gradual turn allowed them to turn out over the exit river. They climbed free of the terrain. The passengers breathed again.

Delbert flew first toward the coastline, then direct to Campbell River. He contacted air traffic control.

"Go ahead Delboat."

"Delboat is inbound to Campbell River with two survivors onboard. Please have two ambulances meet us at the seaplane dock. One will require intensive care."

"Roger. What is your ETA?"

"I am one hour out."

"Thank you. They will be waiting."

The rush Charlie felt when rescued and the apprehension during escape sapped what little energy reserve he had. Almost in a daze, he muttered, "Del."

"What is it."

"Thank you, Del…and Sylvia. Thank…you…"

A tear trickled down his cheek. His head slumped on his chest. Alarmed, Sylvia reached forward and gently pulled it back. She checked his pulse.

"I hope he's not going into shock."

"Looks like he's mainly just exhausted."

"I should have given him more to eat."

"You've done all you can for them both. Getting them out of the airplane. I'll never forget how you picked up Charlie and carried him to his seat. It was unreal!"

"Adrenalin has its uses."

# Chapter 44

As Delbert descended over the Spit, he saw the ambulances. Cars overflowed the parking lot. All boats in the river were coasting off to the sides to give him a clear channel. He landed straight toward the dock and smoothly brought the plane alongside to unload Dan first. The crowd cheered when he opened the window and lowered the ramp.

Medics pulled Dan out and carried him on the stretcher to their waiting ambulance. Doctor Munson joined them in the ambulance and began work on Dan immediately. Cynthia was right behind the medics, tears streaming down her face.

"You found them! Thank God!" She leaped onboard and pulled up the ramp.

Delbert began his patented turn. Charlie woke up during landing. "Cynthia?"

"Yes. You're in good hands now."

"I have been for a couple of hours. Will you call Virginia?"

"Already have. She and Samantha are catching the first plane they can. They'll come straight to the hospital."

"Thank you."

Cynthia turned to Sylvia, "What injuries do you know of?"

"Both legs are broken, neither compound. His right arm was pinned along with the legs. Don't know what damage is involved. They had no water or food for three days. I gave Charlie water and a chocolate bar."

They were docked again. Sylvia got out to give the medics room to lift Charlie out onto a stretcher. Cameras were clicking again. Sylvia had a fleeting thought. *I must look a mess, hair all tangled up, mud all over.* The pictures would prove her right. Their accompanying stories explained why in glowing terms. Cynthia slid over the aisle stand and followed the stretcher to the second ambulance.

Three reporters pressed forward. They all yammered at the same time. Jack McCain stepped in front of them.

"Do you want to field questions now or later, Delbert?"

"We can take a few now."

"Alright, one at a time. You first," he pointed.

"Where did you find them?"

"At a very small lake, not much more than a pond. They flew east of the direct route to sightsee around Mount Waddington."

"They landed there?"

"Not exactly. They were forced to ditch there even though the lake was too small. They slid up the far bank into some cedar trees."

"Why did they have to ditch?"

"I don't know. Dan will have the answer to that."

"You spotted the airplane in the trees?"

"It was hidden by the trees. We spotted the skid marks made by the floats."

"All you saw was skid marks?"

"Yes."

"How could you land safely if they couldn't?"

Delbert chuckled, "This old girl can do a lot of things others can't. We managed to get it stopped on the water. Once Sylvia got our two passengers out and onboard, we taxied a mile or so down the river to a lake large enough for takeoff."

"There weren't any rapids or waterfalls?"

"One stretch of rapids. This is a flying boat in every sense of the word. On the river, it's a boat. On a lake, it's a flying machine."

Jack cut in, "That's enough questions, fellows. These folks are hungry and tired by now."

Left alone at last, Delbert moved the boat to their normal moorage. The crowd applauded again as they came up the ramp. Many congratulated them for the miraculous rescue. Once free, Sylvia drove them home.

\* \* \*

Tired, though still on an emotional high, they settled on soup and a sandwich for dinner.

"They're in good hands now. Let's get some sleep and check on them in the morning."

They laid in bed, still wide awake.

"Honey, there's something that really bothers me."

"What?"

"If I hadn't noticed you giving blood, you might have died trying to save Dan."

"He needed blood to live."

"I love you. I don't want to lose you again and neither do all the people you'll help in the future."

She was silent for a moment. "I'm sorry. I'll be more careful from now on."

He pulled her over onto him in an embrace they both knew would lead to better things.

* * *

Daylight came an hour before they awoke. Sylvia cooked breakfast.

"There's an official letter for you from the coroner's office."

"Hope he's not investigating my death." Delbert tore it open.

"They want me to serve on a coroner's jury that will review that logger's death. The one who felled a tree on himself."

"Are you going to serve?"

"Don't have a good excuse to beg off. Might be interesting. We meet next Tuesday. I'll confirm my participation."

* * *

They learned Dan was still in a coma at the hospital. Cynthia met them in the lobby.

"His vitals are improving. He will be in intensive care for at least another day. We set Dan's leg bones. He's in room four two five. Let's go up."

When they entered the ward, Virginia and Samantha jumped up and charged them. Virginia reached Sylvia first and hugged her. Samantha leaned over and hugged Delbert. Both thanked them profusely for finding the men. Tears of joy flowed. When they finally separated Delbert turned to Charlie.

"How are you feeling?"

"On cloud nine. Don't know if it's from being back in the land of the living or the pain pills Cynthia plies."

"A little of both," Cynthia chimed in.

Delbert turned to Samantha, "Have you seen Dan?"

"They let me in briefly. Poor guy, he looks so weak. Cynthia says they are hopeful that he'll come around. What an ordeal."

"It takes time," Cynthia added.

"If only there's no brain damage. His brain is the center of his universe. Losing his faculties would kill him."

A tear formed at the corner of her eye. Delbert wheeled close and took her hand.

"We must have faith." She nodded feebly.

The conversation turned to a recap of the rescue operation. Virginia, Samantha and Cynthia wanted all the details. The story was tempered by modesty, however, Charlie interrupted frequently to add his perspective. Familiarity with Delbert and Sylvia allowed them to blend the accounts into a reasonably accurate picture. Charlie added a summary note.

"You know it's strange, I think I've lost my fear of flying. I've seen the worst it has to offer and survived. During your turn after takeoff, I sort of enjoyed the suspense of either making it out or becoming tree dwellers again. Even then, I knew you would get us out alive. That confidence renders fear irrelevant."

"Strange. I would have thought the experience would increase your fear. That's great. Dan will be glad to hear it."

"Hey, don't tell him until we see if it lasts."

# Chapter 45

Delbert dedicated the next day to rest and recovery, except for a hospital visit with Samantha. After breakfast, they left Larry to entertain himself and drove to the hospital. Samantha immediately asked the desk nurse if she could see Dan.

"You can do more than that, you can talk to him."

"Is he conscious?"

"Sort of. He's very groggy and not speaking yet but we have him out of intensive care. Doctor Munson put him in a private ward. We don't want to overwhelm him with people and noise until he becomes more alert. Please be gentle and patient with him. Doctor Munson says there should be gradual improvement."

These were not exactly comforting words to Samantha. They sounded more like a forewarning of disappointment. She entered Dan's ward fearing the worst. He was lying on his back staring at the ceiling.

"Hi honey. How do you feel today?"

Slowly Dan turned toward the voice and stared at his wife without expression. Her heart skipped a beat. *He doesn't recognize me.* She put a hand on his arm and stroked it gently. It was all she could do to avoid crying. He continued to stare at her.

"Dan, it's me, Sam." No reaction.

They both remained silent. Thoughts of what life would be like for him if he remained a vegetable raged in her head. She wondered what, if anything, was passing through his mind. A nurse came in and took his vital signs. He ignored the nurse and continued to stare at Samantha. She took his hand in hers.

The nurse said quietly, "We should let him sleep as much as possible."

"Okay."

She stood up to leave and felt an almost imperceptible squeeze on her hand. She bent over and kissed him.

"I love you, Dan. Please rest and get better, darling."

She withdrew her hand and followed the nurse out. He watched her go, then closed his eyes.

* * *

Samantha was crying silently when she rejoined the others in Charlie's ward.

"Is the news bad?"

"He's awake but he can't speak. Just a blank stare. It's so scary. What if that's the way it will be from now on?"

"Have faith," Delbert comforted. Sylvia glanced at him.

"Yes. It's hard though. On the bright side, I think he did recognize me. He seemed to squeeze my hand when I got up to leave."

"That's a good sign," Sylvia exclaimed.

"I hope so. Charlie, how are you today?"

"Fine. A lot closer to walking than Del."

Delbert shot back, "That's a low blow for someone who left my plane a stinking mess. Perhaps I'll leave it for you to clean up. We can roll you down there in a hospital wheelchair."

Virginia chimed in, "Do we need to put a diaper on him?"

"Probably—if he's in the wheelchair for more than an hour or two."

"Okay, I deserve that. Wonder when they will let me go in and see Dad. It might help him remember what happened and know we both survived."

"That's a good idea, son, but I think it has to wait at least another day."

*  *  *

Sylvia and Delbert returned home for lunch since they suspected Larry would go without if they weren't there. They spent a quiet afternoon with him. He continued to soak up everything they could tell him about Cynthia; how well she did in school, how she learned to fly, her time in medical school. He got glassy eyed when they described how she was chosen to give the valedictory address and the great job she did of it. He sounded a little choked up when he spoke.

"You two took what we abandoned and made a wonderful woman out of her."

Sylvia replied gently, "She has your genes, Larry. That determines who she is more than anything else."

"But it took your nurturing."

Delbert interjected, "What the heck. Let's all take credit for how she turned out. There's plenty to go around."

They laughed. Sylvia gave him the loving look she reserved for moments when he defused emotional situations.

* * *

After dinner, Delbert drove Samantha and Virginia back to the hospital. Larry went downstairs to rest.

"You look to be in very good spirits, Mum."

"I've felt invigorated lately. This new job has been good for me, although…"

"Although what?"

"I sometimes feel a little wave of nausea. What could cause that, Doctor?"

Cynthia stared at her. "If I didn't know better, I would say pregnancy."

It was Sylvia's turn to stare, her mouth slightly open.

"Didn't you tell me you can't have children?"

"The doctor said it was highly unlikely that I would get pregnant and even if I did, probably couldn't carry a baby to term."

"As a daughter this is none of my business but speaking as a doctor, does your relationship with Dad make it possible?"

Somewhat embarrassed, Sylvia admitted quietly that it did. Cynthia suggested they drop by the hospital in the morning to find out one way or the other.

Sylvia changed the subject. "I'm concerned about sleeping logistics, we're a bedroom short."

"I'll sleep on the sofa.

"Will you get enough sleep? You go back on day shift tomorrow."

"Tonight, I could sleep on the floor."

# Chapter 46

The next morning Cynthia took Sylvia aside and told her how to administer the test. When it indicated she was in fact pregnant, she suggested they set up an examination with a GYN.

"Please don't tell the others. I want to tell Delbert first—alone. It will be as much a shock to him is it is me."

"I understand."

*　*　*

Dan turned his head when Samantha walked in. A smile formed slowly on his face. Samantha was excited.

"Darling, you look much better today."

She waited for him to say something. Nothing came out. He simply continued to stare at her and smile. She returned it and took his hand again.

"You won't remember it for a while. You and Charlie had to crash-land in what was little more than a pond."

She noticed the smile disappeared at the mention of Charlie's name, replaced by a look of concern.

"Charlie's fine. His legs were broken but they will heal normally. He's in another ward and wants to come and see you soon."

His face became calm again. *He seems to understand what I say even though he can't speak. That's a step forward.* She decided to devote the rest of her time with him on family news. Cynthia came in a little later to check on him.

"Hi Dan, remember me?"

He seemed confused when she listened to his heart with a stethoscope, looked at his wife and back at Cynthia.

"Cynthia's one of your doctors now, dear."

It was hard to tell if he understood.

\* \* \*

Sylvia decided there was another advantage to having a doctor daughter when the GYN agreed to examine her at three that afternoon.

"There's still scar tissue on the uterus wall but in general it has healed well. I think if the placenta attaches properly you stand a good chance for success."

"Thank you, doctor. This is all unexpected...a good surprise, mind you."

She wondered if Delbert would agree after all these years.

\* \* \*

Conversation was more animated at dinner. Seeing a daily improvement in Dan cheered up Samantha. Only Sylvia remained quieter than usual. Cynthia glanced at her from time to time. Delbert noticed it too but decided she was simply deferring conversation to the other women.

Virginia announced, "I should get back home and rescue the kids from my mother or more likely, rescue her from them."

"If you wait one more day, you can take Charlie with you. His stamina has returned. He is processing food normally. We can release him tomorrow afternoon."

"In that case, sure."

Delbert chuckled, "He'll get out of town and leave me with that mess to clean up."

"You know I'm the one who will end up doing it," Sylvia retorted.

Samantha chimed in, "I want to have Charlie spend time with Dan tomorrow before he leaves."

\* \* \*

Sylvia cuddled next to Delbert in bed. That wasn't unusual, yet Delbert sensed something and asked what bothered her. She kissed him.

"I don't know how to break this to you gently—I'm pregnant."

He drew back. "What?"

"Is that bad now?" she asked, suddenly frightened.

"No, it's wonderful. Are you sure?"

"Yes."

"After all this time. I had given up hope."

"You should have had the faith you admonished Samantha about," she chided with a laugh.

After the initial shock, Delbert was excited. He pulled her into a hug.

"Carrying it to term will be a challenge but the doctor thinks there's a good chance."

"We need to leave that in the hands of fate."

"Or the hands of God."

He laughed. "Either way it will take the same amount of time to find out."

A happy couple kissed and hugged, for the moment too excited to sleep.

# Chapter 47

Delbert rolled into the modest court room at nine o'clock on Tuesday. Roderick Hanes, the coroner, introduced himself and welcomed the six jurors plus one alternate.

"Thank you all for agreeing to serve. As you may know, we are required by law to convene an inquest into any death not attributable to natural causes or common afflictions known to be terminal. Our case is one Nathaniel Bengstrom, known familiarly as Ned. Mister Bengstrom was killed by a tree he appears to have felled upon himself. Your job is to determine if his death should be ruled an accident, suicide or homicide. Any questions?"

Silence.

"Alright then. An autopsy was performed on the victim. You will each be given a copy of the report. However, I will summarize the findings in more easily understood terms. Death was caused by asphyxiation due to an inability to breathe because of the weight of the tree pressing on his back. There was evidence of a blow to the back of the head but that was not fatal. The victim lived for a short period of time after the tree fell on him. His facial expression was characteristic of someone gasping for air. You will see that when you view the body."

One of the jurors gasped. "We have to view him?"

"We prefer you do but it's not essential that all of you do. If you have serious qualms, you may decline. In this case, the body does not appear mutilated."

The man shuddered. Everyone else followed the Coroner into the morgue to view Ned's frozen body. Delbert got the impression that Ned looked more angry than fearful. Perhaps he was angry at his own stupidity.

Back in the courtroom, the coroner advised them there would be only two called to testify since no one witnessed the accident. Delbert thought it premature for him to call it an accident before hearing from them. The first was the crew foreman, a grizzly elderly bowlegged man with at least a day's growth of beard and a visibly powerful body. It was doubtful that any logger would want to cross him.

He described the lay of the land and the gully Ned was in at the time of the accident. "He was sort of hemmed in without a lot of escape routes. Even so, he must have misread the lean to fall it on the only good way out."

The coroner asked, "So you think he misdiagnosed the tree situation and accidentally brought it down on his only escape route?"

"Misdia—what?"

"Incorrectly sized up the tree situation."

"Yeah, he must have brought it down on hisself. There was no one else there."

There were no other questions. Hanes thanked him and called the next witness to be sworn in.

"Do you, Joseph Beaumont Carson, swear to tell the truth, the whole truth, so help you God?"

"I do."

"Mister Carson, you were Ned's partner and the person who found him first, correct?"

"Yes, your honour."

"No need to call me an honour. I'm just a simple coroner."

Some in the jury laughed.

"Now would you please tell us everything you know about what happened to Ned?"

"Well, the boss described the layout. I was on the camp side of a ridge that crossed the head of Ned's gully. We normally make contact once an hour, but I let it go longer since it was a hard climb over the ridge, and I could hear his chain saw easy enough.

"That afternoon when I paused between trees, I didn't hear anything. Thought we happened to take a break at the same time. I started a cut on the next tree, then paused again. Still nothing. That's when I decided to go check on him. As soon as I reached the top of the ridge, I could see things were bad for him.

"I rushed down, grabbed his saw and bucked the tree trunk on either side of him. Then I pulled him out with the intention of giving him artificial resus—resus…"

"Resuscitation."

"Yes. But I didn't because his body was cold and stiff. I ran back to camp to get help instead."

"Did you try to figure out how it happened?"

"When we went back I looked things over. It was hard to tell exactly but it looked like maybe Ned thought the tree was leaning into the hill and tried to fall it that way. Looked like the tree twisted as it fell. When you're standing on a slope it's easy to misread the lean. That's why I carry a little plumb bob with me. Most every tree on a slope leans down the hill. Ned should have known that."

Delbert spoke up. "Just as a rough average, about how many trees do you fall in a shift?"

"Oh...I fall about two an hour with the limbing and all."

"How long had Ned been a faller?"

"Hmm, round eight years that I know of, maybe longer."

"That means he's fallen over twelve thousand trees successfully."

"If you say so. You're a lot quicker with the arithmetic than me." That brought a faint laugh from the others.

"Strange that he would make such a blunder after all that."

"Yeah, well, Ned was a little simple in the head, poor bugger...and there was a gusty wind that day."

Delbert continued to study Carson. Something gnawed in the back of his mind. *I'm missing something. What is it about you that bothers me, Joseph Beaumont Carson? Your name's worse than mine. The school bullies would have a field day, Joseph Beaumont...Joe Beau—Jobo! Ned was a big man. It's him!*

The coroner had dismissed him. He was walking away toward the door. Delbert said "Jobo" loud enough for him to hear. Most people would not have noticed a reaction but Delbert saw a minute hesitation in his step.

As he opened the door, Jobo turned and scanned the room. Everyone was either talking or looking down except the guy in the wheelchair who still watched him. Their eyes locked for a second, then he turned and was gone.

Hanes summed up, "That's the extent of information we have available and it all points to an accidental death. Could I have a show of hands if you agree?"

All hands but Delbert's went up. "Does that mean you don't agree, Mister Pillage?"

"Afraid so, sir. In view of Ned's experience level and the lack of an explanation for the bruise on the back of his head, I think further investigation is warranted."

Hanes sighed. "What possible further investigation do you suggest?"

"Well, a forensic specialist and an expert faller could go over the scene in detail, search for a cause for the bruise, check that all the cutting was done with Ned's saw, determine what prompted Ned to make those cuts, that sort of thing."

"You sound like a conspiracy theorist, Mister Pillage. I don't think we can afford to send people out on a wild goose chase. We'll just take the will of the majority and declare Ned's death accidental."

With a resigned grimace, Delbert left.

# Chapter 48

As he drove to Mabel's, Jobo pondered. *Where have I seen that cripple before?* Suddenly, it came to him. *On the ramp at the dock!* He made a U-turn, headed to the river and collared the first worker he encountered.

"Tim, you know that cripple in the wheelchair that comes around here?"

"You mean Pillage?"

"What's his name?"

"Delbert Pillage. That's his seaplane over there."

"Delbert Pillage. Has he lived in Campbell River long?"

"I think he just moved here this summer."

"Where did he come from?"

"Don't know."

*If he grew up here, he might know they used to call me Jobo but it looks like he didn't. That means he may have connected me with the kid in Vancouver.* He decided to try the office.

"Jake, I'm trying to get in touch with Delbert Pillage. Want to rent his plane. You got his address?"

"Should be on his account info. Let me look."

"Thanks."

"Here it is—forty-five Ridgeview Place."

He drove to within a block of the house and parked. *It looks over that steep bank.* He backtracked to the first road leading down to the highway and turned south. Parked where he estimated Delbert's house to be, he surveyed the bank. Too steep to climb. On the other hand, it would probably kill Pillage if he could push him over it. And he could come down here an finish him off if necessary. The whole thing would look like an accident. Satisfied, he drove back up to stake out the house.

* * *

Larry sat in the front room when Delbert rolled in.

"The girls went shopping. Asked me to tell you they'll be back by two."

"Okay. I'm going to open a can of soup. Want to share some minestrone and a sandwich?"

"If you don't mind, some soup sounds good. Don't want to trouble you for the sandwich."

"It's as easy to make two as one. Tuna okay?"

"You folks are real kind to put me up. I hate to be a sponge on you."

"Larry, you brought Cynthia into the world. She's brought a world of happiness into ours. You're family to us."

"You and Sylvia teach people how to live right. Wish I could have learned from you twenty years ago."

Delbert laughed it off and moved into the kitchen. The words did create a warm feeling he preferred not to show.

* * *

After lunch, Delbert rolled around the house down to the lawn in front. Some peaceful time to himself might help sort out a strategy for dealing with Jobo. However, his thoughts returned to Sylvia. They both wanted a child but he realized it was much more important to her. She felt guilty in the early days for depriving them of children because of her botched abortion. Did she still feel that? It hadn't come up in years. Worry didn't help. They needed to simply let events unfold.

For a while he simply sat and stared at the ocean. Relaxation suffused his body. When his thoughts returned to Jobo, he broke the issues into two parts. First, was Joseph Beaumont Carson really Jobo the murderer? Second, if he was, how could sufficient evidence be found to convict him?

The flinch, minute as it was, convinced him the man had been called Jobo before. There could be many people in the world nicknamed Jobo. *What convinced me he is the guilty one? When his eyes locked on mine from the doorway, they were the cold-blooded eyes of a killer. And he searched for the person who called him — me. And Ned matched the description of his partner. I think he's the one.*

That gave rise to the question of evidence. Could the victim's girlfriend pick him out of a line-up? And if she did, was that enough? Not likely. Ned could have fingered him. He probably felt pangs of guilt. Jobo had to silence him and he did. Hanes might find evidence of that second murder if only he would order an investigation immediately. What else was there to connect Jobo to the first murder. Perhaps someone in town could place him in Vancouver at that time. Slim chance of that.

He needed professional advice. When Cynthia returned, he would get her opinion on taking his conclusion to Jack. Jack might be able to pressure Hanes into further investigation and he could approach his Vancouver counterparts for advice. In the meantime, he let his mind go blank again to enjoy the sun's warmth and the hypnotic quality of the ocean below.

An active mind never remains blank long. Delbert's thoughts turned to his air car concept. He pictured the design, a circular vehicle that looked like an upside-down saucer. Is that where the mystique of flying saucers comes from? In his, the outer ring was a giant fan. Not a conventional fan with a hub at the center. More like a ring consisting of the outer two feet of the fan blades. He called it a ring fan for that reason. They would run around the vehicle on tracks. There would be two rings running in opposite directions so the counter-rotating blades would prevent the vehicle from spinning around.

The feature that pleased him most was the method of powering them. An engine in the center would drive the equivalent of a propeller shaft. The inner rim of the ring fans had teeth, on the bottom of the upper ring and top of the lower one. The drive shaft had a cylindrical gear with teeth that mated those on the rings. When the shaft spun, it would drive the upper ring in one direction and the lower in the opposite. A simple way to generate necessary lift without the stresses of a helicopter type of blade.

The ring fan would be used strictly to lift the vehicle. Control of its attitude and forward motion would come from four smaller electric fans that could be rapidly aimed using actuators. They would keep the vehicle stable in gusty winds, provide forward motion and control turns. Electronics would take care of all that. The pilot (or driver) need only give directional and speed guidance.

He visualized himself flying the air car. It dawned on him that he could have two smaller engines driving the ring fans.

That way if one failed, the second would supply enough lift for a safe landing—maybe even permit completion of the trip. The sun made him drowsy. It became hard to distinguish conscious thought from a dream.

# Chapter 49

Jobo cruised slowly down South Murphy onto Ridgeview Place. He saw no one at the Pillage house so he went to the end of the street and turned around. On the way back, he spotted Delbert sitting on the front lawn, his head slumped forward. There was no one else in sight. A perfect opportunity.

He parked in front, quietly closed the car door and walked around the west side of the house. Delbert appeared all alone. He sneaked close, then with a dash grabbed the wheelchair, spun it around and pushed it toward the bank. Delbert woke with a start, realized his peril, and threw himself out onto the lawn just in time. The wheelchair went careening down the bank. He pulled himself back from the edge.

Jobo aimed a kick at his head. When Delbert saw it coming, he barely had time to block the main force with his arm. It rolled him on his back. Another kick was on its way. He grabbed the boot and pushed up. It grazed the side of his face. He held onto the foot and twisted. Jobo was thrown off balance. He hopped on his other leg trying to pull his foot free. With upper body strength Jobo never anticipated, Delbert held on.

Suddenly, a second man charged into Jobo. Delbert pushed his foot away. Already off balance, Jobo staggered backwards down the slope. When a foot found only air, a shocked look crossed his face as he disappeared over the edge of the bank.

Delbert dragged himself further from the edge, still groggy from the first kick. He looked up at Larry.

"Thanks."

"What happened, Delbert? Who was that?"

"A murderer. He tried to push me down the bank. You saved my life. He may climb out."

"I'll get something to deal with him."

He ran with adrenalin-fed energy to the house and returned with a shovel, gasping for air.

"I'll deck him if he shows a head over the edge."

Delbert would have preferred he call the police, but Jobo might appear while he was gone. They waited.

\* \* \*

Sylvia and Cynthia were animated as they drove home.

"I'm so excited about having this baby."

"That's wonderful. It seems like the years were needed to ensure sufficient healing of your uterus."

Silvia laughed. "You and Delbert might not agree but I think God was keeping track of my progress."

"I won't disagree. You deserve the joy of a child."

They noticed the unfamiliar car as they drove into the garage and decided it must be someone visiting a neighbour.

"We're home." Sylvia announced. No answer.

Cynthia stuck her head into the living room and saw Delbert lying on the lawn with Larry standing over him, shovel in hand. She screamed and raced down the stairs.

She yelled as she charged them, "Larry, put that shovel down!"

Delbert raised his hand. "Hold on, Thia. He's protecting me."

"What—from what?"

"Jobo."

"Jobo? The Jobo?"

"I'm ninety percent sure he's the one who killed Tom in Vancouver. He figured out I was onto him and tried to push me over the bank. He succeeded with my lower half."

Larry chimed in, "I'm going to deck him when he climbs out."

Cynthia looked from one to the other.

"I guess that makes me a freak of nature."

Delbert gave her a quizzical glance. "How's that?"

"I've got two dads."

Larry interrupted his vigil long enough to turn and say, lips tremulous, a catch in his voice, "Thanks, Cynthia."

Sylvia patted Cynthia gently on the back of her shoulder.

"Are you hurt, dear?"

"Just bruised a little."

"And scraped," she said looking at his cheek, "I'll call the police."

While she ran inside, Cynthia gingerly approached the drop off. "You won't need the shovel. He's not coming out."

Delbert twisted around, dragged himself over and peered down the bank. Jobo's lifeless eyes stared skyward, his head jammed against his shoulder by a large boulder half buried thirty feet down.

As the crisis passed, Larry's adrenalin rush dissipated. He crumpled to the ground. Sylvia saw him first and called his name. Cynthia turned and rushed to him. He was conscious, wheezing, trying with little lung function left to get oxygen. His skin was ghostly pale.

"Help me get him up to the house."

The two women lifted him, surprised at how light he now seemed. One on each side, they carried him to the deck. He said one word, "chair", they sat him in the first one.

Delbert dragged himself away from the bank, frustrated by his inability to walk or even crawl. The women came back for him.

"Sit up, dear. Put an arm around each of our shoulders."

He did as told. They stood up in unison, then made a saddle under him by grasping each other's hands.

"I feel like an Asian potentate," he quipped on the way to a second chair on the deck.

A siren announced help arrived. Moments later, Jack ran around the side of the house. He stopped short, confused, when he spotted the four of them on the deck.

Cynthia explained. "Delbert discovered Tom's killer, Jobo, who then tried to push Delbert over the bank. With Larry's help, they fought him off and he fell down instead. He's halfway down, wedged against a boulder, probably dead."

Jack ran down to look and returned shaking his head. "What made you think he's the killer?

"His name is Joseph Beaumont Carson—Jo Bo. He flinched on his way out of the coroner's court when I called that out to him. He homed in on me as he turned to close the door. I'm pretty certain he's the one."

Jack glanced at Cynthia. "What a pair those two are...or were in his case."

Cynthia blanched. "John's brother?"

He nodded. They were distracted by a painful wheeze from Larry. Cynthia went to him, took his hand to check his pulse. A little blood trickled from his mouth. He was much worse than she had thought.

"We need to get you to the hospital."

Jack stood behind her, ready to help. Larry shook his head, gazed out at the ocean, then back to Cynthia and up to Jack. With a clarity of thought brought by death's approach, he gasped, "Take...care... of her."

"I will."

His eyes travelled back to Cynthia.

"Forgive...me...for leaving...you."

"I forgive you, Dad."

Sylvia gave Delbert's hand a gentle squeeze. Larry felt a peace envelope him. *I didn't accomplish all I wanted but it doesn't matter because I created this wonderful woman.* The last thing he saw was her beautiful, tear-stained face.

Cynthia realized the pulse stopped. She gently closed his eyes. Jack held her. She leaned against him and turned a lost look toward Delbert and Sylvia.

"Come here, dear."

The four held hands in silence. Finally, Delbert broke it.

"Thia, you often thank us for saving your life, though I prefer to think of it as helping you to save your own life. In any case, if you persist in thinking there's a debt involved, it was repaid in full when Larry saved mine."

###

# Other Books by Sandy Graham

### Life Shattered

Delbert Pillage hides his intelligence through early school years to reduce harassment. Only Sylvia Cairns sides with him and a love is born. His true ability is uncovered in high school and early entry into university separates them. While he is in a summer air force training program, a tragedy pushes her out of his life. He matures into Canada's youngest jet test pilot with all the risk that entails. In this emotion packed story, with his two are shattered … or are they?

### Life Rescued

Delbert must search for a new mission in life. He finds not one but two. Can he rise to the challenges, given his disability? Will he ever enjoy any kind of normal lifestyle? This sequel blends good and bad human behavior with intense emotion, adventure and sexual immorality.

### The Pizza Dough King

Dino Parelli tells his life story from high school to his dying breath. It's a life marked by successes and tragedies as Dino struggles to win the girl of his dreams, build a business around an unusual niche market, deal with personal losses and cope with old age deterioration. A heart-warming story of enduring love and a lesson in personal and corporate ethics.

## Murder – On Salt Spring?

How can there be serious crime on this small island in 1952? Too hard to escape with only a ferry and besides, everyone knows everyone else. In minutes, secrets become common knowledge. Yet, Carl Jenson is found in bed with a knife sticking out of his chest.

Big city detective Mattie Carlyle is sent out to help laid back Cal Lockhart investigate the murder. At loggerheads from the start, can their growing attraction lead to common ground? And can the murder be solved? Can you solve it?

## Speak For Me

In a world torn between democracy and dictatorship, can America survive the onslaught of authoritarianism and become once again a beacon of democratic leadership? Emergence of a powerful propaganda machine places the answer in doubt.

A musically gifted extrovert, John McEwan becomes embroiled in this battle, dragging Emma Simon, a deaf introvert, in with him. Forces against them turn violent, driving them into seclusion, tearing them apart, and destroying their rapidly growing company. In a dramatic role reversal, Emma reveals how a strong individual can rise in the face of crises. This emotion-packed novel, at times heart-wrenching, at times heart-filling, lights a path to a brighter future.

## A Quiet Rampage

A memoir of my life …so far to age 80.

**For more, please visit www.SandysPen.com**

Manufactured by Amazon.ca
Bolton, ON